W9-AYD-205

"There's so much I want to say . . ." I said, caressing her back, pressing my lips to her neck.

"Shhh," she murmured. "Talk later." Her voice was husky, the way I remembered it. My lips found hers tentatively, touching softly at first, then giving way to the pent up passion. I slid my hand inside her nearly open robe and felt a sound escape from somewhere in the back of my throat. My hand cupped her breast and she shivered, then moaned. I moved down, kissing her throat, her collarbone, working my way to the taut, full nipples. When I took one into my mouth, Erica cried out.

The robe fell to the floor as I continued my descending exploration of the body I remembered so well. Her skin was smooth and warm, and I could hear her heart beating in cadence with my own. My fingers brushed the glossy black triangle of curls and Erica bit my shoulder, making a noise that both frightened and excited me. We were still standing, barely, on trembling legs. She'd never looked more beautiful, I thought.

LOOKING FOR NAIAD?

Buy our books at
www.naiadpress.com

or call our toll-free number
1-800-533-1973

or by fax (24 hours a day)
1-850-539-9731

7TH Heaven

KATE
CALLOWAY

THE NAIAD PRESS, INC.
1999

Copyright © 1999 by Kate Calloway

All rights reserved. No part of this book may be reproduced or transmitted in any form or by any means, electronic or mechanical, including photocopying, without permission in writing from the publisher.

Printed in the United States of America on acid-free paper
First Edition

Editor: Christine Cassidy
Cover designer: Bonnie Liss (Phoenix Graphics)
Typesetter: Sandi Stancil

Library of Congress Cataloging-in-Publication Data

Calloway, Kate, 1957 –
Seventh Heaven : a Cassidy James mystery / by Kate Calloway.
p. cm.
ISBN 1-56280-262-3 (alk. paper)
I. Title.
PS3553.A4245 1999
813′.54—dc21

CIP

For my father — the most supportive man I know,
my mom, for teaching him how to be that way,
Carol for being Carol,
and Fat Cat, probably the happiest creature
to walk this earth. Well, waddle it, anyway.
I miss her.

Acknowledgments

A heartfelt thanks to my friends (again!) for taking the time to read and critique a work in progress: Murrell, Linda, Carolyn, Deva, and especially Carol who keeps me honest! Thanks, too, to Christi Cassidy for her encouragement and unerring eye, and to all my friends and family for their continued support. Finally, thanks to those readers who have offered such kind feedback and support in their letters, reviews and notes on the Internet. And to those of you who asked for Erica, well, get ready. E.T. is back!!!

About the Author

Kate Calloway was born in 1957. She has published several novels with Naiad including *First Impressions*, *Second Fiddle*, *Third Degree*, *Fourth Down*, *Fifth Wheel*, and *Sixth Sense*, all in the Cassidy James Mystery Series. Her short stories appear in *Lady Be Good*, *Dancing in the Dark*, and *The Very Thought of You*. Her hobbies include cooking, wine-tasting, boating, song-writing, gardening, and spending time with Carol. They split their time between Southern California and the Pacific Northwest; setting for the Cassidy James novels.

Chapter One

It looked like a band of carnies had descended on Cedar Hills overnight. Colorful tents and awnings shaded food-laden tables and makeshift game booths along the water's edge of the usually quiet lakefront park. A country western band was already in full swing on stage and though just past noon, people of all ages were dancing. The beer garden was packed, Frisbees and kites filled the perfectly blue summer sky, and as I stood gawking at the scene I realized nearly everyone in town, and a good many outsiders as well, were in attendance.

"Purdy good for the first one, huh?" Tommy Green said, his elfin features scrunched as he scanned the crowd for likely dance partners. "You wanna brewski? I'm buyin'."

"No, thanks, Tommy. I'm supposed to keep my palate cleansed until the contest. Speaking of which, there they are."

I pointed toward a purple banner announcing the First Annual Rainbow Lake Clam Chowder Cook-Off and headed toward it. Tommy kept in step, bouncing along beside me on the balls of his feet. As usual, he was dressed in Levi overalls with no shirt beneath, and a blue Mariners cap turned backwards. He only stood about five-feet-four, and his muscled arms bore burn scars from a boating accident. What made him irresistible to women was beyond me. Maybe it was the perpetual grin he wore or the way his eyes crinkled with mischief. Whatever it was, by the time we reached the Clam Chowder Cook-Off tables, he'd attracted a whole bevy of giggling teenagers who were begging him to come play on their football team.

"Aw, now girls. I can't go playing tackle football with you all. You might hurt me." He winked at the girls, then added, " 'Sides, I'm supposed to protect Miz James here from bribery and other such tomfoolery. She's one of the oh-ficial judges of the cookin' contest, and I'm supposed to keep her honest."

I rolled my eyes at this exaggeration and watched as the girls trailed away.

"Thank you, Tommy. I feel much safer now."

He grinned. "No problem, Cass. It's true, you know. People could bribe you. If one of these fancy chef types wins this thing, his restaurant will get wrote up in that *Coast Magazine* and then his business will start boomin'."

What he said was true, which was why so many of the good restaurants up and down the coast had entered the contest. It was also why, as judges, we were not allowed to know whose chowder we were tasting until after we'd picked the winners. We had one hour to decide, between twelve and one o'clock. Then the chowders were up for grabs to the general public. The winners would be announced at four.

The other six judges had already arrived and were working their way down the roped-off tables. Bystanders stood among the chefs just outside the ropes, watching the judges' expressions expectantly. The pots of chowder were numbered and judges kept notes on scorecards. Three of the judges were well-known chefs who had chosen not to enter the contest, two were local dignitaries, the other a lucky citizen like me who just loved good food. I was pretty sure that the only reason I had been selected was because everyone in town knew I was a glutton. No matter. I was both pleased and honored to participate. Besides, I was starving. I'd limited myself to a few pieces of toast and a small glass of orange juice that morning, and the aromas emanating from the steaming pots were almost more than I could bear.

I signed in, donned my judge's pin and strode confidently toward the first entry, my scorecard tucked into a back pocket. I ladled a bit of chowder into one of the tasting cups and just as I raised the spoon to my lips, I scanned the crowd watching me. Sure enough, one pair of eyes seemed more intent on me than the others. So much for anonymity. Entry number one no doubt belonged to Mike Tally, owner and chef of The Crab Pot in Florence, a favorite restaurant of mine. I looked away, embarrassed that I'd just broken the contest rules and tried diligently to concentrate on the chowder itself. Creamy and smooth, with generous chunks of clam that to my liking were a bit too chewy. I made a note on my scorecard and moved to the next entry.

Despite myself, I couldn't help glancing at the onlookers. There amid the chefs and cooks were many of my friends and acquaintances watching with interest. But when I saw the beaming blue eyes of Sheriff Tom Booker practically brimming over, trying to get my attention, I knew that his wife, Rosie, who stood beside him and refused to look in my direction, was contestant number two. Damn! This wasn't working at all. I was cheating and I didn't want to! I loved Rosie. She was not only a good friend, but a great cook. Her chili rellenos were the best I'd ever had. But what if I hated her chowder? What if I didn't? What if it was the best of the lot? Would people think I'd cheated because the Bookers were my friends?

Resolutely I looked away, nibbled on a cracker to neutralize my palate, then dipped into Rosie's chowder. It was marvelous. The clams were not as plentiful as in the first entry, but they were sweet and tender. Specks of yellow dotted the surface and melted in my mouth, and I savored the rich, buttery flavors that held, to my surprise, a hint of tarragon. This was not traditional chowder, and Rosie, if anything, was traditional. I resisted the urge to peek up at her, willing myself to concentrate on another taste. Delicious. It was all I could do to stop myself from ladling a whole bowlful and settling down for lunch. Instead, I made notes on my scorecard, kept a neutral face, refusing to look up at the crowd again, and moved on to the next steaming pot.

By the time I'd tasted all sixteen chowders, I could no longer remember what the first one had tasted like. Many of the judges had moved back through the line, tasting their favorites a second time and I did the same. I'd narrowed it down to three chowders. As other judges turned in their final selection, I went back and forth, tasting the three chowders again.

"Come on, Cassidy. You're just trying to get a free lunch!" someone shouted. I looked up at the sound of Tommy Green's voice and did a double take when I saw who was standing beside him. To my dismay, I felt myself blush. Erica Trinidad, as striking as ever, was smiling back at me.

"Just pick one!" someone else shouted, getting into the mood. "We're starving!"

I realized that I was the last judge to finish and was holding up lunch for the rest of them. I searched the crowd until I found Rosie, watching me serenely. Booker, who still stood beside her, had a funny look on his face, but he wasn't looking at me. He was looking at Erica Trinidad.

Oh, what the hell, I thought. If they told me I could only have one bowl of soup to eat for the rest of the day and I had to pick one, I'd pick Rosie's. *So just do it!* I smiled back at Rosie, wrote my selection and pushed it through the little opening inside the ballot box. The whole crowd cheered and someone moved the ropes away. I barely had time to escape before they rushed the tables.

"Now I'll take that beer, Tommy," I said, glancing at Erica.

"I'll be right back," he said, trotting away.

"You took your time," Erica said, appraising me with eyes even bluer than I remembered. I did a quick mental check of my appearance, glad that I was wearing the blue shirt that Martha always said matched my eyes. But why should I care? I ran my hand through my short blonde hair, idly wondering if it looked as windswept from the boat ride over as it felt. One thing about living in a house only accessible by boat — no matter how good I might have looked when I left, by the time I docked, my hair was in disarray. But from the look in Erica's eyes, I could tell that she liked what she saw, and I felt myself beginning to blush.

Refusing to acknowledge my discomfort, I returned her gaze, boldly assessing the changes in her since we'd last met. Erica's dark hair was cut in layers, framing high cheekbones and a wide mouth. She wore a white sleeveless cotton blouse that showed off finely toned biceps and a dark, California tan. The top two buttons were left undone, revealing a glimpse of cleavage. Subtle but unnerving. She looked more like a successful lawyer than a romance writer, I thought. But her books were known worldwide, and recently she'd begun working on screenplays as well.

Keep your cool, Cassidy, I warned myself. So, naturally, I came out with something completely inane. "It was much more difficult than I thought. I guess I'm not cut out for this judge stuff."

"Oh, I don't know. We've both had our moments of being judgmental."

Just like that. After not seeing each other for more than a year, without so much as a good-bye the last time she'd left, she came out with a zinger like that.

"Yeah, I guess we have." If it was a fight she wanted, I wasn't going to rise to the bait. I just wanted to relax and enjoy the afternoon. Besides, she was right. We'd both had our moments. "You been in town long?"

"A week or so. I came to get some writing done. And to think. It's impossible to think in L.A. I couldn't resist coming today, though. Looks like the whole town is here."

"You still making movies with your director friend?" I kept my voice light and neutral. Or I tried to. A little anger might have seeped out.

Erica laughed. "No. That flopped a long time ago. The movie, I mean. The director friend lasted a few months longer. How about you? Still seeing the shrink?"

Despite myself, I flinched. Maggie and I were no longer seeing each other, but it wasn't something I necessarily wanted Erica Trinidad to know. Besides, this time, Erica had nothing to do with the problems between Maggie and me. This time, it had been Maggie's ex-lover who had come between us. That the lover died more than a year ago, didn't really matter. She was there just the same, driving a wedge between us. And the further apart we grew, the more we were able to see that we each had other unresolved issues, feelings for people in our past that prevented us from completely committing to each other.

"Not at the moment," I said evenly, keeping any

emotion out of my voice. There was no need for Erica Trinidad to know the details of my love life.

"Hope you like micro-brews!" Tommy said, handing us each a plastic cup brimming with amber ale. Erica and I tipped our cups in mock salute, then drank thirstily. My palm felt sweaty against the cold plastic and I wondered why, after all this time, she could still have this effect on me. I'd gotten over her years ago. I certainly wasn't interested in revisiting old mistakes.

"Thought you'd never decide!" Booker said, sneaking up behind me and pounding me on the back. "Hope you chose well!"

"Hi, Tom. You remember Erica Trinidad."

Booker rolled his eyes at me and extended a hand to Erica. " 'Course I remember her. You think I've gone senile? Old maybe, but I still got my marbles. How are you, Erica? Last I heard you were making movies. Though they sure had you on the wrong end of the camera. California must agree with you. You're as brown as a bear."

This was Booker's way of reminding me, in case I'd forgotten, that Erica had left me for the movie director. This wasn't lost on Erica, either, but she smiled graciously.

"And honey still drips from those lips, Sheriff. Good to see you again." They shook warmly, but with a mutual wariness I could sense. They had always liked each other, but with reservation.

"You want a beer, Sheriff?" Tommy asked. "I'm buyin'."

"What'd you do? Win the lottery?" I teased. Tommy was a generous, good-natured guy, but he wasn't known for saving money and was more apt to borrow a buck than lend one. He smiled at me mysteriously, like maybe he *had* won the lottery, and crossed his muscled arms, making the burn marks stand out in the sun.

"Why aren't you dancin' with the girls?" Booker asked him.

"I been bodyguardin' Cassidy, 'case someone tries to bribe her."

Booker threw back his head and laughed, making his white moustache twitch. It must have tickled his nose, because he smoothed it down with both hands, still chuckling. In his late sixties, he was ruggedly handsome with laugh lines at the corners of his blue eyes and a weathered, tanned face that could have belonged to the Marlboro Man. The black cowboy hat he wore completed the image.

"What's so funny?" Tommy demanded. "It could happen."

"I know, I know. Thought about trying it myself, that's all. Some of these fancy-schmancy Chef-Boy-R-Dees would just have a conniption fit if one of these little old Cedar Hills gals beat them out and won the thing."

"Like Rosie," I said.

"Yeah, like Rosie," he agreed.

"If you'll excuse me," Erica said. "Nature calls."

"I'll walk you over," Tommy said. "Gotta go myself."

Booker and I watched them walk toward the restrooms, Erica with her long-legged, confident stride, Tommy bouncing along beside her.

"I think Tommy's smitten," I said.

"Wouldn't be the only one." He paused, making I sure I didn't miss his meaning. "Surprised to see her?" he asked.

I looked at him sideways. "As a matter of fact, I am. Why?"

"Saw the look on your face, that's all. Seen that look before, as I recall. Said to myself, 'Oh boy, here we go.' "

"What's that supposed to mean?"

"Cassidy, your face is an open book and you're as predictable as a dog chasing a bone. You're smart about most things, but when it comes to that woman, you're plumb dumb."

"I am not!" I knew I sounded about eight years old, but I couldn't help it.

"Mark my words. Erica Trinidad is trouble. She can't help herself. God gives someone that much beauty and talent, they're bound to make trouble. Just happens, that's all. No fault of hers. No fault of yours. Just hate to see it happen all over again, that's all."

"Well, you needn't worry yourself on my account. That was a long time ago, Tom. A lot has happened since then. Things have changed." I took another drink of my beer. I'm not sure who I was trying to convince more, him or me. I changed the subject. "Anyway, your face isn't exactly a closed book, you know. You think I couldn't tell which soup was Rosie's? Damn, you might as well have shouted it out."

"What do you mean?"

"Come on, Tom. You were practically beaming at me. But don't worry. I would have picked it anyway. It really was the best. That tarragon was a brilliant addition."

"Tarragon?" His puzzlement was genuine.

"Rosie didn't use tarragon?"

"In clam chowder? You're kidding, right? Rosie?"

I felt my cheeks start to flush. "Then why on earth were you trying so hard to get my attention when I tasted the second entry?"

"Because, you idiot, I'd just seen Erica Trinidad and thought you'd be tickled to see her. Just because I said she was trouble, doesn't mean I don't like her. You never looked up again so I gave up. You thought Rosie would put tarragon in her chowder? Don't tell me you picked that one!"

Before he could finish, a panicked call for help shattered the light banter around us. We looked toward the restrooms and my stomach plummeted. Even from a distance I could see the terror etched on Erica Trinidad's face. Her voice cut through me like an arrow. "Somebody's just killed Tommy!"

Chapter Two

I beat Booker there by about two strides. Others had rushed forward, and a crowd stood gawking as Erica performed CPR, pressing her lips to Tommy's, willing his lifeless form to breathe. Booker crouched down and pressed his fingers to Tommy's throat.

"I think there's a pulse." He turned and yelled, "Who's got a cell phone? Call nine-one-one. You! Run to the stage and call for Harry Manchester. Or any doctor. Move aside, Erica. Let me take over." He nudged her aside and pressed his ear to Tommy's chest. "Come on, kiddo. Hang in there," he mumbled to Tommy, who looked, as far as I could tell, already gone. I felt my throat clamp and willed myself not to burst out sobbing. I watched as Booker gently lifted Tommy's head and heard a collective gasp from behind me. The back of Tommy's head was matted with blood, a three-inch gash open and pulsing.

"Jesus!" Booker muttered. "Gimme something. A towel. A T-shirt!"

Someone pushed forward, pulling off his yellow tennis shirt in one swift movement as he kneeled beside Tommy. His bare back gleamed in the sunlight. "Will he make it, Sheriff?"

Booker looked up, his eyes pained. "Don't know, Professor. He's breathing. Thanks." He grabbed the shirt and pressed it tenderly to Tommy's head.

"Here come the medics!" someone shouted.

"Outa my way! I'm a doctor!" Harry Manchester roared, pushing his way through the crowd. In the distance, a siren sounded. The ambulance was on its way. Erica looked shaken and moved toward me as the space around Tommy closed in with those who could help him more than we could. The bare-chested professor backed away too, noticing as if for the first time the blood on his hands.

"You okay?" I whispered to Erica. Her face was pale and I was afraid she'd faint.

She made a movement with her head, not quite a nod, but an attempt at one. "He said something." Her voice was almost inaudible.

"Tommy? Said something to you?"

"Shh. Not here." She looked around anxiously, her earlier confidence replaced by vulnerability and fear. I couldn't help myself. I wanted to take her in my arms.

By now the sound of the sirens was deafening.

Booker's new deputy, Newt Hancock, pushed us all back to make room, and we had to watch from a distance as Tommy was lifted onto a gurney and rolled into the back of the white ambulance. Booker climbed in after him, and they roared off toward Highway One. The closest hospital was in Reedsport, fifteen miles North of Cedar Hills. I only hoped the ambulance would make it on time.

"You the one that found him?"

Erica and I wheeled around and faced Newt Hancock. He was in his early thirties, I guessed, with dark lazy eyes, black glossy hair combed straight back, a stylish goatee and a silky moustache which he stroked as he spoke.

"Yes," Erica said.

"I'll need to take a statement just as soon as we finish cordoning off the area," Hancock said. "You wanna come sit down? You look a little shook." His voice was soothing. Slow and easy.

"We need to get to the hospital and check on Tommy," I said.

"It's Cassandra, right?" His eyes narrowed, long lashes nearly hiding his pupils.

"Cassidy."

"Right. Cassidy, you can go on ahead if you want, but I'll need to talk to this young lady now. Sheriff said to get her statement and that's what I intend to do."

He stared at me, almost seductively, gracing me with what can only be described as bedroom eyes. His laid-back, all-the-time-in-the-world drawl could've lulled a bear into hibernation. I made a show of looking at my watch.

"This won't take but a minute," he said, moving off toward the restrooms in a leisurely stroll. He stopped, flicked something off of his pant leg and looked over his shoulder at us. "Just wait over there. Oh, and don't talk to anyone else before I get back."

I walked Erica to a shaded bench and sat down beside her, though the last thing I felt like doing was sitting. My stomach was in knots and my fists were clenched with anxiety.

"What happened?" I asked, ignoring the people looking in our direction. In the distance, the band started to play again, but it seemed as if a pall had been cast over the entire festival. People spoke in hushed tones and I knew that as fast as news traveled in Cedar Hills, the whole town would soon know what had happened.

"I came out of the bathroom and saw him crawling toward me from the men's side. I rushed over and saw the blood. His eyes were awful — they were rolling back in his head — but I know he recognized me." Erica's lower lip trembled and I reached over, taking her hand in mine. "He could barely talk, and what he said didn't really make sense."

I waited. Then, not able to stand it any longer, I blurted, "What did he say?"

Erica closed her eyes as if wanting to get it just right. "He said, 'Don't tell anyone.' Then I said something like, 'It's okay, Tommy. You're going to be okay,' and I started to call for help but he grabbed my hand and whispered something. I could barely hear him. He said, 'Can't trust any of them. You find it, Erica.' 'Find what?' I asked. By then he was having trouble breathing and his eyes closed. He said,

'Flowers.' And then he passed out." Erica began crying softly and I put my arms around her, fighting back my own tears.

"You sure you're going to be all right?" Hancock said, startling us both. He stroked his goatee and peered down at us. Even in uniform, you could tell he was a sharp dresser. His slacks were creased and his boots were reptilian, either snake or alligator, I thought. Like Booker, he wore a black Stetson, but where Booker's looked well-worn and lived in, Newt's was shiny and new.

I knew from what Booker had said that Newt was the nephew of a prominent judge in New Mexico, an old friend of Booker's. Actually, I wasn't sure how thrilled Booker was to have him. Booker was used to running his own show, doing things his own way. But the kid seemed content to walk along in Booker's shadow, wasn't overly ambitious and didn't come charging in wanting to change things, like Booker had feared. In fact, though he never said so, I got the feeling Booker thought Hancock was on the lazy side, more interested in pursuing his off-duty pleasures than in law enforcement. I watched as he leisurely took out a notepad and began asking Erica the routine questions. It took several minutes for him to get down to the crucial issue.

"You see anyone else in the vicinity?"

"No. Just Tommy. He was crawling away from the men's bathroom. Maybe there were other men inside who could tell you more."

"Well, there musta been at least one, but I doubt he's gonna tell us much, right?" He lowered his eyelashes and tried a smile but it was lost on Erica. "So he was still conscious when you found him. Was he able to talk?"

"No, I don't think so. I tried to revive him, but . . ." Her voice trailed off. "That's when I yelled for help."

"So he didn't say anything at all. And you didn't see anyone else." He put one boot up on the bench beside her and used his hand to wipe off a few blades of wet grass.

"Not very helpful, I'm afraid," Erica said.

"Please, Deputy. If that's all you need for now, we need to go check on Tommy."

Hancock looked over at me, and his eyes closed momentarily. He was either bored or I was trying his patience. "How about before you went into the ladies' room? See anyone hanging around outside?"

Erica paused, unsure. "I don't think so. I wasn't paying much attention. There was someone in one of the stalls on the women's side, but I never saw her. I mean she was gone before I got out. Maybe she saw something."

"Any sounds? You hear Tommy make a yell or anything?"

"No, not at all. I could still hear the band from inside, but no voices. The last thing Tommy said to me was, 'I'll wait for you outside.' " Erica's voice trembled and I knew she was on the verge of tears again. But even in this state of extreme distress, she was a talented liar. The last thing Tommy had said to her was 'flowers.' Obviously, she did not want to share this bit of information with Hancock.

"How about you, Cassandra? You see or hear anything that might explain why someone would attack Tommy Green? Was he acting funny in any way?"

"It's Cassidy, Newt. And no, he seemed his normal, cheerful self. If anything he was in a really good mood. He'd been looking forward to this festival all week."

But his question made me think, and I knew I wasn't answering completely honestly. It was true that outwardly Tommy had seemed the same. But there were little things that, put together and in light of what happened, might mean something. I thought back and took a silent inventory. Tommy had been looking for girls, yet he hadn't asked a single one to dance. Had he been on the lookout for someone else instead? Even when the girls found him and practically begged him to play football, he declined. In fact, he'd stuck to me like glue, supposedly to protect me from "bribery." But maybe it wasn't me who needed protecting. Maybe Tommy was using me as *his* bodyguard. He'd even waited to use the restroom until someone else decided to go. Did Tommy know someone was out to get him? And why was he suddenly eager to buy everyone a beer? Had he come into money? Did someone else know about it? Had he been robbed?

"You think of something, Cassidy?" Hancock was peering at me, his dark eyes probing.

"Uh, sorry. No. I'm afraid my mind isn't focusing very well. Do you think he could've been robbed? Was his wallet missing or anything?"

"We'll have to check with the sheriff on that. Did he have a wallet on him? Can you describe it?"

"Just a regular leather wallet. He carried it in his left back pocket. He carried a little tin of Skoal in his right." For some reason, this detail got to me and I started to choke up again. "We have to go now. I really need to be with Tommy."

"I suppose we're all finished here for now." He reached up and lightly traced his moustache. "If you think of anything else, though, please get back to me."

"What a piece of work," Erica mumbled as I steered her toward the parking lot. Outside the yellow tape a few onlookers still stood gawking at the scene where Tommy's blood had stained the dirt in front of the restroom.

"Look," I whispered, pointing to a spot just beyond the men's restroom.

"What?"

"The flower bed." I started in that direction but Erica pulled me back.

"We can't look now, Cass. Everyone will see us." She was whispering but her tone was fierce. "He said not to tell anyone and not to trust anyone, and I don't know what the hell he was talking about but I'm not going to let him down."

I looked at her and was taken by her beauty. Her blue eyes were glistening with tears and her cheeks were flushed with emotion.

Without saying another word, I took her hand and together we headed for my Jeep Cherokee parked at the marina.

Chapter Three

Tommy was in the operating room, which was a good thing. That meant he was still alive. But the look on Booker's face was grim.

"I called his mother in Texas," he said. "Not sure she'll make it until tomorrow. You think of anyone else we should notify?"

"Gus?" I suggested. Gus Townsend owned the marina where Tommy worked. He was one of the few locals I hadn't seen at the festival.

"Already tried. His wife said he's up in Florence at some boat auction. Any girls?"

I gave him a look that despite his mood made him laugh. "Okay, okay. Dumb question. Besides, by now the whole town knows. I'm surprised there aren't more people here already. I at least thought the Bailey boys would be here. He's been chumming around with them pretty regular."

"They're in the downstairs waiting room with a whole carload of girls. Rosie's there, by the way. We'd have been here sooner but your Deputy Do-little wouldn't let us go. Then the nurse from hell wouldn't let us up until we said we were family. Have you talked to the doctor?"

"No one's said anything yet. But it doesn't look good, Cass. You need to know that."

I nodded, feeling the lump in my throat tighten. "Any idea what happened? Was he robbed?"

Booker narrowed his eyes at me and tugged on his moustache. "Wallet was missing. He was hit from behind with something, probably more than once. Something with a hook or point, I'd guess, from the shape of the wounds. Either someone just wanted to knock him out, nab his wallet and run and they did more damage than they intended, or else someone intended to kill him and took his wallet as an afterthought." Booker raised one eyebrow and drilled me with a steely gaze. " 'Less you got another idea?"

"Well, it does occur to me that maybe it wasn't me he was bodyguarding, as he put it, but the other way around. Maybe he knew someone was after him."

"What makes you think so?"

Erica shot me a warning and I shrugged. Booker glanced over at her but her face went blank.

"It's just that he was sticking like glue today. He even followed Erica to the bathroom. Like he didn't want to be alone."

"Hmph," Booker started to pace the little waiting room. "You give your statement to Hancock?" he asked Erica, watching her closely. Booker prided himself on reading expressions.

She nodded, looking miserable. "I told him I saw Tommy crawling out of the restroom, but before I could reach him, he collapsed. When I saw the blood, I started yelling for help."

"But he was conscious when you first saw him?" The same thing Hancock had asked.

Erica nodded, then lied. "But only for a second."

She was saved from further fabrication when the door opened and a green-smocked surgeon in matching cloth booties entered the tiny waiting room.

"The Green family?" she asked. Her Asian eyes looked mournful.

"I'm Sheriff Tom Booker. This is Cassidy James and Erica Trinidad. We're friends of his. His mother is on her way from Texas. Right now, this is as close to family as he's got."

The surgeon nodded and glanced at Erica and me, then back to Booker. "The swelling in his brain was such that our only option was to induce a coma and wait for the swelling to go down. This may take days or weeks or longer. There's no guarantee it will work. Sometimes, with an injury of this nature, healing occurs rapidly and we can begin to address other concerns. You should know, however, that there is the possibility of impairment to his cognitive skills. It's too soon to tell. At this time the best we can do is wait and hope and pray."

"But he'll live?" I asked, feeling myself fill with unexpected hope.

"There is always a chance. It depends so much on the patient. His will to live, his state of health, his resiliency. There are so many variables with something like this . . ."

"He'll live," I said. I had never known anyone more resilient, with more will to live, more zest for life than Tommy. If that's all it took, he was as good as healed.

The doctor smiled at me, but her eyes were sad and some of my optimism faded away. "These next twenty-four hours are crucial. We'll know more tomorrow."

"Thank you, Doctor." Booker shook her hand. Erica and I followed suit, though I was numbly going through the motions.

"I need to get back," Booker said. "I do hope to God Newt had the sense to secure the scene properly."

"He had yellow tape around the whole area and was keeping everyone back when we left."

"Good. Listen. There's no point in you girls hanging around here. The best thing for Tommy now is to get some rest. I imagine they'll move him to post-op and then ICU."

"Someone should be here when his mom arrives," I said.

"I'll ask Rosie to wait. She'd insist on it anyway. She has a knack for this kind of thing. Let's go down and tell the others the news."

We took the stairs, none of us wanting to endure the silence of the elevator. We were all raw with emotion. Erica was still pale. I felt like someone had sucker-punched me, and Booker looked like he'd been up all night. When we reached the downstairs waiting room, the crowd had grown to nearly twenty. Some of the girls were clutching flowers from the gift shop. Booker spoke briefly to Rosie, who nodded, then he held up his hand and addressed the others. He spoke in a low voice, repeating only some of what the doctor had said. Strangely, he left out any hint of optimism.

"So how long will he be in the coma?" Bart Bailey asked. He was one of Tommy's buddies, an auto mechanic with red frizzy hair and a smattering of freckles across his face. His twin brother, Buck, would've looked just like him, save for his cleanly shaved head and propensity for facial piercing. The stud on the tip of his nose was particularly charming. Bart looked like an overgrown Tom Sawyer. Buck looked more like a beefed-up Hell's Angel.

"Could be a long time, Bart. No visitors for now. We'll know more tomorrow. Those of you who brought things, if you want to leave them with Rosie, she'll be sure they get to his room, once he's assigned one. The best thing any of us can do for the time being is just pray."

People nodded solemnly and a few of the girls in back started to cry, handing Rosie their flowers before filing out into the sunshine. It seemed incongruous to me that the sun should still be shining. Had it only been a few hours since I'd shared a beer with Tommy and Erica? It seemed a lifetime ago. I asked Rosie if she wanted us to stay with her, but she insisted we get some rest, so we walked Booker to his cruiser.

"You want to tell me why you just painted a picture bleaker than hell? Even the doctor said there was *some* hope."

Booker tugged at his moustache and looked over my shoulder at some of Tommy's friends who were still milling around in the parking lot. "You said it yourself, Cass. Maybe someone was after Tommy for some reason. If they wanted him dead, Tommy probably knows why. And there's a good chance he knows who tried to kill him, even if he *was* hit from behind. You think whoever did that is gonna be happy to know Tommy might pull out of this?"

"You're saying you think they might come back and try to finish the job once they find out he's alive?"

"It's been known to happen. As long as Tommy's in a coma, he's probably safer than if he wasn't. Rosie knows not to let anyone near him but his mama, at least for now. This might just buy me a little time to figure out what's happening."

I started to say something but Erica, who was standing right behind me, poked me in the back.

"Anything we can do to help?" I asked.

"Get her back home and fix her something with a little kick in it. She looks like she could use it. You too, for that matter. Rosie will let us know if anything changes."

"Thanks, Tom." Seething, I led Erica back to the Jeep and climbed in. "Booker's my friend, Erica. We can trust him, for God's sake."

"Tommy said 'Don't trust *anyone.*' He didn't say, 'Anyone except the following people.' He meant *anyone.*"

I looked at her sideways and started the engine. "You sure you can trust me?"

She reached over and punched me in the arm.

"Ow!"

"You deserved that. And anyway, if I didn't think I could trust you, I wouldn't keep coming back to Cedar Hills, would I?"

"What's that supposed to mean?"

"Ah, forget it, Cass. Just drive. Sometimes you make me crazy."

I pulled out of the hospital parking lot and floored it.

"Where are we going?"

"Tommy's. Somebody's got to feed his cat. Might as well be us. Besides, I think we ought to have a look around. Don't you?"

Tommy Green lived on the north end of town in an old double-wide mobile home that abutted Rainbow Creek. Just across the creek was a cow pasture and beyond that the forest. His only neighbor was a quarter-mile back toward town where the pavement ended on Creek Street. We bumped along the final stretch.

"Quaint," was all Erica said when we stepped out of the Jeep.

"Nice and private. Good view, too," I said, feeling oddly defensive about Tommy.

"Probably grows pot back here. Who would know but the cows?"

"Probably. Come on. I'll bet you ten bucks it's unlocked."

A few minutes later, and ten bucks poorer, I went back to the Jeep for my lock picks. I tended to keep them handy, though I knew that having them near only encouraged my fondness for breaking and entering. It was a bad habit and a dangerous one, but one I felt drawn to time and again. Probably a burglar in my last life, I thought, clicking the pick into place and gently easing the front door open. Erica was grinning.

"What?"

"You get off on that, don't you?"

"Shh! Come on!" I pushed the door the rest of the way open and tiptoed into the mobile home. I wasn't sure why I was sneaking around. There were no neighbors to hear us and Tommy lived alone. We stood in the entryway and listened, looking around. The place was empty.

"Besides the cat, what are we looking for?" Erica asked.

"I'm not sure. Anything out of the ordinary. Something that might tell us what Tommy's been up to lately. Here, kitty, kitty," I called softly.

"Probably keeps the cat outside during the day," Erica said. "What's its name?"

"Pepper. She started out as Paprika because she's orange, but Tommy's allergic to her and decided to call her Pepper." Erica looked at me blankly. "Because she makes him sneeze."

"Oh. Right. Pepper! Here, Pepper!" She moved off toward the kitchen and I walked through the house, room by room, looking under beds and tables, wondering what it was that Tommy had wanted Erica to find. Would we find it here? It would've helped if we'd known what to look for.

I was surprised at how neatly Tommy kept things. I'd expected casual disarray with beer bottles strewn around the place, dirty underwear hanging from doorknobs, that kind of thing. But except for a haphazardly stacked pile of books on the floor next to a worn ottoman, the place was fairly tidy. Not immaculate. The sinks could have used some cleanser and the furniture some dusting, but for a single guy, the place wasn't bad. There were window boxes with red begonias outside the bedroom window and a hanging fern in the corner. He'd even made his bed, a waterbed with red silk pillowcases, and when I looked beneath the spread, matching sheets. I smiled and understood the general neatness of the place. Tommy brought girls here, and regularly.

I stood in the center of Tommy's bedroom, staring into the open closet, almost feeling guilty for this invasion of his space. But someone had attacked Tommy, maybe even tried to kill him, and I wanted to find out who. But where to start? Who would want to hurt a harmless, good-natured marina attendant who liked to drink beer, smoke a little weed and flirt with the girls? Had he flirted with the wrong girl? I didn't doubt for a minute that a married woman would be attracted to him. It had happened before. Maybe someone's husband had found out.

But the thing that was bugging me, I thought as I began going through the pants pockets in Tommy's closet, was his behavior at the park. It was as if he'd known someone was after him. And that smile when I'd asked if he'd won the lottery. Like maybe he had. Tommy was up to something and whatever it was, it had nearly cost him his life.

"Found her!" Erica said, making me jump. She was holding the orange tabby against her chest, stroking its thick fur. "Oh, sorry. Didn't mean to startle you. You find anything?"

"Uh, not yet. This may take a while. Why don't you take Pepper outside while I look around?"

"Hey." She walked across the room and handed me the cat, stepping so close to me that I could smell the perfume on her neck. "I want to find out what's happening as badly as you do. He trusted me enough to tell me something was wrong. I don't think he'd mind my helping you find out what it is." The whole time she talked, she stroked Pepper who was now kneading my chest and purring loudly. Erica's hand brushed against my cheek and when I looked into her eyes, her gaze held mine. "We made pretty good partners before, Cass. No reason we can't try it again."

Which partnership was she referring to, I wondered. The one in which we'd worked together to find her uncle's killer? Or the one that came later? I stepped back, putting the cat gently on the floor. I did not want to think of that kind of partnership with Erica.

"I'm not sure where we should start," I said, turning away. "So far, I've found two condoms and a five-dollar bill. Not exactly enlightening. I guess since he mentioned flowers, I might as well take a look in that window box outside. Why don't you gather up those books by the chair." The truth was, I needed the fresh air. I left her standing in the bedroom, a faint smile playing on her lips.

If only I knew what to look for. A key? Tommy had said that Erica should find "it," and then he said "flowers." I started out gently, but before long, I'd pulled the begonias completely out of their container and was scooping the dirt out in handfuls, making a complete mess on the porch. It didn't take long to realize that the only thing hidden in the window box were a couple of cutworms and a snail. I dumped the dirt back into the box and tried to reset the begonias in their place. At the sound of an engine, I wheeled around and saw a truck approaching, still a block away.

I rushed to the front door and yelled for Erica to get out quickly. Then I returned to the porch and did my best to sweep away the dirt with my foot while I straightened the begonias. Erica came rushing out the front door, a bulging pillowcase held in one hand, the cat held against her chest. She ran to the Jeep, stuffing the pillowcase inside. Then she climbed into the front seat and waited, stroking Pepper to calm her.

I stood by the front door, away from the mess that was still visible on the porch outside the bedroom window, and waited for the green Ford pickup to come to a stop.

"Hey," Bart Bailey said, pushing a sweat-stained baseball cap back from his carrot-colored locks. "What are you guys doing here?" His brother, Buck, got out of the driver's side and leaned against the hood of the truck. He seemed bigger than Bart. The bald head made him look meaner, too. That and the nose stud and eyebrow rings.

"Came to feed the cat. It was the least we could do."

"Damn nice of you," Buck said, squinting into the Jeep where Erica held Pepper up in plain sight. Why did I feel something wasn't right about these guys? Could be the gun rack in the back window of the truck, I thought, though that was hardly an unusual sight. Could be I was just cynical by nature. "Hey, aren't you the one that found him?" Buck walked toward the Jeep and put his hands on the passenger's side window. Erica stared back at him, refusing to flinch. "Heard he was conscious when you found him. Talking and stuff."

"Guess you heard wrong," she said. "He was conscious when I saw him crawling out of the bathroom, but by the time I reached him, he was out."

"Too bad," Buck said, pushing back from the window. "If you'd reached him in time, he coulda told you who did it." He made an exaggerated show of cracking his knuckles, and I couldn't help wondering who had told the Bailey brothers that Tommy had been conscious. Aside from Booker and Hancock, Erica had only told me. Then again, maybe they were just making assumptions.

"What are you guys doing here?" I asked, knowing they had as much right to be there as we did.

Bart spoke up, sounding much more civilized than his brother. "My brother wanted to get a few of our things since it might be a while before Tommy gets out. Tommy borrowed some shovels and stuff."

"*If* he gets out," Buck said.

"He's getting out," Bart said, his freckles standing out more noticeably. "Tommy's going to be fine."

Buck shrugged, his head gleaming in the late-afternoon sun.

"Probably should wait to ask his mom, though," I said. "She's probably going to be staying here while Tommy's in the hospital."

"Shit, she doesn't know what's his and what's ours! Fuck that! We'll get it now." Buck started toward the garage. Like Tommy, he wore overalls with no shirt underneath. The muscles on his back bulged as he tried to heft the garage door. A metal padlock held the door firmly in place.

"What the fuck?" Buck hissed.

"Door's locked, bro." Bart seemed embarrassed by his brother's behavior.

"Dude never locks the door." Buck stood up, his face red from the exertion. "Fuck this. Let's go!"

Bart leaned out the passenger's side window, an apologetic grin on his freckled face. "If you guys take Pepper away from here, the whole place will be running with field mice. Tommy's gonna be ticked if he's got mouse turds in the house."

"He isn't gettin' well, dumbfuck. Get used to it, man. Dude is gone." Buck climbed into the truck and slammed the driver's door.

"You don't know that for sure, Buck!" Bart turned to his brother and for once, Buck backed down, literally sliding down in his seat before turning the ignition.

"Right. Whatever."

"You want me to tell Tommy's mom to be expecting you? She should be here soon." This was a lie, but I thought it might stop them from returning right away.

Buck leaned out the window. "Naw, forget it. We don't need that stuff right now, anyway. It can wait." Buck backed around and tore down the road, sending dirt flying in all directions.

"Charming guys," Erica said. "Especially the bald one. Let's get out of here before anyone else shows up."

"What's the hurry? It might be interesting to see who else does show up. If whoever hit Tommy knew he hid something, they're probably still looking for it."

"That's why I want to get out of here. You know those books you wanted me to get? There's something you need to see, Cass. Come on, Pepper. Let's put you back inside so you can guard for mice. We'll come back tomorrow to see how you're doing."

I watched as Erica carried Pepper back in, kissed the cat on the forehead, then stepped back onto the porch, locking the door behind her. Trouble, I thought. But very beautiful trouble.

Chapter Four

I pulled into my usual spot in the marina parking lot and we hurried down the ramp to the water. Erica's turquoise speedboat, which she'd bought as part her late uncle's estate, was moored just a few slips from my open-bow Seaswirl. She followed me through the channel, past the still-crowded county park where the festivities were still in full swing and out into the open water. I opened the throttle and fairly flew across the surface, sensing Erica in my wake. I was nervous about inviting her back to the house. But my place was closer than hers and I was anxious to look at Tommy's books. When we pulled up to my dock, neither of us talked much and it occurred to me that she might feel as awkward as I did.

It felt strange having Erica back in my house, but apparently I was the only one who thought so. Panic and Gammon welcomed her with ankle rubs and obscene purring, and Erica made herself right at home, sprawling on the couch in the living room like it belonged to her. I busied myself with closing windows. The wind had come up on the lake and the house was chilly. I went out back to get a load of firewood, though I knew in part I was just taking the opportunity to clear my mind.

The first time Erica Trinidad had come into my life, I'd been taken completely by surprise. I was living alone on the lake, having moved away from my job and friends in California, away from the memories of my long-time lover who had died in my arms. I hadn't expected to ever fall in love again. In fact, I didn't much care if I even went on living. But my best friend, Martha Harper, had dragged me to the Oregon coast, talked me into learning a new craft, that of private investigation, and little by little, despite myself, I had started to heal.

Living alone along the rugged shoreline of Rainbow Lake in a house accessible only by boat was just what I needed. No neighbors to jolly me out of my grief. No television to clutter my mind. I watched the deer graze on the front lawn, watched the blue heron and osprey fish the lake and slowly felt myself beginning to mend. Just when I had started to feel like I could make it on my own, along came Erica Trinidad and suddenly I was no longer content in my isolation.

Everything about our time together was intense.

She had loved with abandon, and to my surprise, I experienced a passion I'd never dreamed was possible. Then, while I was still trying to catch my breath, Erica was offered a movie deal on one of her books and she was off to Hollywood, leaving me dazed and confused. By the time she decided to return, I was with Maggie. Although I'd loved Maggie and cherished our time together, I'd never quite been able to erase my feelings for Erica — not the passion I'd felt for her, not the anger at her sudden departure. Now, as I gathered more wood than I needed, I tried to stuff the feelings back down where they belonged.

"You want a cup of tea or something?" I asked.

"I distinctly heard the sheriff say you should give me something with a little kick in it and you offer me tea?" She looked up, grinning. "Come on, Cass. I know you've got a bottle or two of good wine squirreled away somewhere."

Actually, I had one open. "Chardonnay?" I asked, not waiting for an answer. I poured us each a glass and walked to the couch.

Erica raised her glass, her gaze locked with mine. "To Tommy's recovery," she said.

"To Tommy." I lifted the glass to my lips and swallowed, still holding the gaze. I felt the heat rush to my cheeks. Damn her! I turned away, set my glass on the coffee table and went to light a fire.

"It'll be cold as soon as the sun goes down," I explained unnecessarily, stacking kindling on the grate. Erica started taking books and papers out of the pillowcase, spreading them in front of her on the floor. Panic began inspecting them too. I was tempted to come look over her shoulder but gazed out at the lake instead. It had been a long time since Erica's uncle's speedboat had graced my dock. It bobbed on the water, an iridescent turquoise reminder of the obnoxious man who'd been murdered four years ago. He'd always looked silly in that boat, I thought. But somehow when Erica drove it, she didn't look silly at all.

"I was surprised when you told me to get these books," she said. "Tommy doesn't exactly strike me as the bookworm type. But then I saw what they were. Listen to these, Cass. *Hidden Treasure on Rainbow Ridge. West Coast Miner's Lost Gold. Myths and Fables of the Oregon Forest.* These were checked out of the Cedar Hills Library a month ago. They're overdue. He copied down excerpts in this notebook. Then there's these old newspaper clippings that he's photocopied and clipped together."

I added a couple of logs to the fire, made sure they caught, then went to retrieve my wine.

"See this one? *Logger Finds Clue to Hidden Treasure.* I'll read it to you. 'Bob Thurston, better known as 'Bout-a-mile Bob, may have just stumbled on what locals believe could be a clue to the famous hidden treasure of Rainbow Ridge. According to Bob, he was headed back to the logging camp near Rainbow Ridge when he was forced to stray from the trail.' " I came over and sat down next to her, peering over her shoulder as she read in a fairly credible backwoods twang.

" 'I come across a mother bear about yea high and a coupla cubs and decided to skeedaddle afore it made a supper outta me. I stepped off the path and kinda sidewinded my way outta there, but afore I knew it, I was a little lost. I decided to follow the settin' sun 'cause I knew the camp was west of where I'd started.

'Bout a mile, or so, I come across what look to be a red bandana flappin' from a tree branch. This were a puzzlement, since I swore I was the first human being to set foot in them woods for a purdy long time. My curiosity got the best of me, even though the sun were settin' and a storm were brewin' and I best be gettin' back to camp, but I shimmied my way up a bit and tried to grab hold of that bandana. Seems it were tied onto something aside from the branch and I saw it were some kind of pouch. I couldn't reach it cleanly, but I made a lunge for it and pulled myself up, but the pouch was good and stuck. I managed to worm my hand inside it and got a good hunk of parchment afore I fell back to the ground. That's when I done this to my ankle.' " Erica, who'd really gotten into Bob's twang, stopped and took a sip of wine. "Isn't it funny how they just left all this bad grammar in back then?" she asked.

"It probably didn't sound as funny to them as it does to us. Go on."

Erica continued reading. " 'When Bob finally limped into camp in the pouring rain several hours later and told his story to the logging crew, they were skeptical. But when he showed them the torn parchment he'd managed to rip away from the leather pouch, their eyes widened. Bob Thurston is not a proud man and doesn't mind admitting that he cannot read. When the logging chief, Jake Mays, read the words on the parchment aloud, Bob nearly fainted. It seems he'd found the long-lost clue left by the famed West Coast Miner who hid his wagonload of gold in the early part of the century. The problem was, he tore the parchment right down the middle, so until someone finds the other half, the clue remains a mystery. But in case you're thinking of being the one to find it, know this: That night's rain washed out any tracks Bob might've made and for a full week now, the logging crew has been unable to find the spot where Bob says he found the clue. "It's about a mile from here," he says over and over again. It could be the joke's on us. Maybe 'Bout-a-mile Bob's just pulling our leg. Of course, if he can't read, how the heck could he write a note, albeit half of one? Just a little food for thought from your friendly *Depot* Reporter.' "

"When was that written?" I asked.

"Nineteen-twenty. It was in something called the *Depot Monthly*. Didn't there used to be a train depot in Cedar Hills?"

"Sure was. But that was eighty years ago. And the note, if it really did exist, has to be older than that. Don't tell me you think Tommy's been out looking for a century-old piece of paper in hopes of finding buried treasure, for God's sake?"

"Wouldn't put it past him. I mean, anyone else, I'd have doubts. But Tommy? It kind of fits, don't you think?"

I hated to admit it, but it did. "What's the rest of this stuff?"

"More articles. Looks like after this last one was published, another one came out about the 'gold rush' for the red bandana. And look at this. Bob Thurston's obituary. They more or less repeat the story. Says he spent the rest of his days looking for the other half of the note. No wonder they wrote books about it."

"Here's a picture of the note," I said, flipping through one of the books. Written with a fancy cursive, the note itself was intriguing, if not very helpful. It read:

"I, Mason Ordane of Seat . . .
this note to be true and belonging to my . . .
their rightful belongings to the gold and . . .
in the event the injuns succee . . .
from this marker due nor . . .
then down the ravine and . . .
another twenty paces un . . .
right down along the purp —' "

"Check these out," Erica said, handing me two maps. One was of the general Cedar Hills area, the other a detailed map of logging roads and camps. He had circled a few of the spots in red pen. One of them was the logging camp near Rainbow Ridge.

"Okay. So Tommy's out looking for gold. That I can buy. But you don't think for one second he actually found something?" I got up and went to stoke the fire. The light outside was fading to dusk and I suddenly realized I was famished. I'd made a pot roast the day before and had enough leftovers for a week. I placed the roasting pan in the oven and poured us each another glass of wine.

"Now this is weird," she said, holding up a color printout from a Web site.

"The whole thing is weird, Erica."

She ignored my comment and perused the printout. "Looks like Tommy was suddenly interested in purchasing a gun. Wonder why he didn't just go buy one? Why over the Internet?"

"I'm surprised Tommy even knows how to use the Internet. Let me see that." Sure enough, Tommy had downloaded a home page offering a variety of firearms for sale. I noticed the date the document was downloaded. "Did you say those books were checked out a month ago?"

"Over a month ago. They're overdue. Why?"

"Because this was downloaded last week. First he starts collecting info on this lost gold, then a month later he starts getting info on guns. Then someone attacks him and he tells you not to trust anyone and to find something in the flowers." Somehow, I thought if I repeated the sequence often enough, maybe it would start to make some sense. I let the paper fall to the floor and went to check on the pot roast.

"You think Tommy found the red bandana?" she asked, coming to peer into the oven. I felt her closeness, breathed in that damned perfume and closed my eyes, willing myself to ignore her presence.

"No, Erica. The chances of Tommy finding something that no one has been able to find for a hundred years is a bit far-fetched. I think he might have looked for it. But I don't think there's a chance in hell it even still exists."

"So what did he hide? And why did someone attack him?"

I looked into her blue eyes. A dark tendril of hair had fallen against her cheek and I resisted the urge to brush it away, to touch her cheek. "I wish I knew, Erica. Come on. If you set the table, I'll go find us some red wine. Maybe something will come to us over dinner."

The pot roast was falling apart, just the way I liked it. Erica acted as if she hadn't eaten in weeks and spoke with her mouth full, garbling her words.

"Say that again, in English?" I teased.

"Maybe he didn't find the note. Maybe he just found the gold."

"Right, Erica," I said, rolling my eyes. "But there was so much of it he couldn't carry it all and then he couldn't find his way back again. This is exactly how these old myths get started. A hundred years from now they'll be talking about Tommy Green and his lost treasure."

Erica looked chagrinned. "I don't claim to know the answers, Cass. I'm just posing questions." She helped herself to more wine and I wondered if the rosiness in her cheeks was from emotion or alcohol. I did not want her to get to the point where she couldn't drive her boat back to her uncle's place. It's *her* place, I silently reminded myself. It had been hers for four years, even if she did only visit a couple of times a year.

"You gonna be okay to drive?" I asked. It was easy to get lost on the lake at night. Erica's house was only a couple of coves over but in the dark, it could be tricky. She looked at me and a smile crossed her lips.

"Afraid if I get tipsy I might let you take advantage of me?"

"Very funny. I'm afraid you might plow that fancy speedboat into Alder Point. You want some coffee?" I got up, mostly to hide the blush on my face.

"No thanks, Cass. Here let me get the dishes. Why don't you go call Booker and find out what's happening? Then I'll leave you safe and sound, no barriers broken."

I should have left it alone, but I couldn't.

"What barriers are you referring to?"

"Oh, God, Cass. You know. All those barriers you

put up to protect yourself. You couldn't let yourself cry today even though your heart is breaking for Tommy. You couldn't allow yourself to be pleased to see me, even though your face lit up. And you can't allow yourself to touch me, even though every time I get near you your eyes practically beg me to kiss you."

Open-mouthed, I looked at her, not sure if I wanted to slap her or laugh. Or cry. Everything she said was true and I hated her for it. I shook my head, unable to let myself speak.

"I just wonder what you're protecting yourself from?" Her eyes were boring into mine. "What are you afraid of? If you cry, you think someone's going to think you're weak? If you kiss me, you think someone's going to think you're easy? Are you afraid of me, Cass? Or are you afraid of yourself?"

"Some people drink too much and they get silly or maudlin. Unfortunately, Erica, you just get ridiculous." I went into the bathroom and shut the door quietly behind me. I didn't come out until I heard the speedboat roar to life and race away from my dock.

Chapter Five

I slept fitfully and awoke before dawn, my heart racing. The events of the previous day came rushing back like a wave. After Erica had left, I'd called Booker, but Tommy's condition hadn't changed. His mother and an aunt had arrived from Texas around ten, and taken a motel room in town. Booker had promised to call me if there was any news, but I felt uneasy and decided not to wait. I got out of bed, startling Panic and Gammon, who were unaccustomed to getting up in the dark. After making coffee, I called the hospital and asked to talk to the night nurse in ICU.

"His vitals are stable," she reported.

"But he's still in a coma?"

"Yes. The good news is, there doesn't seem to be any sign of infection yet."

"Is anyone there with him?"

"Not now, dear. He's only allowed hospital-supervised visits by family members. Don't worry. We're monitoring him very closely."

Booker had probably insisted on the supervision part, I thought, as a way of protecting Tommy. "It's for the best, dear. What he needs right now is complete rest. That and time to heal."

I thanked her and hung up feeling a little better. If he'd survived the night, maybe he'd pull out of this all right.

Outside, the sky was beginning to lighten, the fog lifting off of the lake like cotton candy. The water was glass. I watched a great blue heron cruise the shoreline, its white tufted beard inches from the water. Panic nuzzled my ankle, reminding me that she hadn't had breakfast.

"Okay, you little muskrats. What will it be? Kitty Gourmet or Kitty Gourmet? You're in a rut, you know."

I opened a can of their favorite food and dished it into two bowls. Gammon, nearing twenty pounds, tended to scarf up all of hers in a few minutes, then go to work on what was left of her sister's. Panic didn't seem to mind. She spent her day hunting and supplemented her diet with moles and other unfortunate creatures. Gammon preferred to spend the day sprawled on the front porch in a patch of sun, watching the world pass her by. She was the more beautiful of the two, with large gooseberry eyes and dark brown spots on luxuriant, fawn-colored fur that made her valuable to cat thieves and breeders alike. Panic had finer, softer silvery fur and a tail as long as her sister's belly was round. Half-Egyptian Mau, half-Bengal, they made a striking pair.

"Watch for bears," I said, letting them out through the sliding glass door. It wasn't bears I was worried about, though. There were plenty of other predators that might not hesitate to take on a pair of cats. In the last year I had seen raccoons, mink, otters, porcupines, a mountain lion, bald eagles, osprey, bears and of course, deer on my property. The deer did the most damage. They munched everything they could reach and I'd finally had to build a greenhouse in back, just so I could enjoy a few of my own vegetables.

I watched the two cats tiptoe through the front lawn toward the lake, then went through my daily exercise routine, practicing karate kicks until my thighs ached, working out some of the tension that had built up over the last twenty-four hours. I knew it wasn't just anxiety over Tommy. The scene with Erica had been a fitting ending to a horrible day and try as I might, I couldn't get her words out of my mind. What gave her the right to talk to me like that? To look at me like that?

Exhausted and sweaty, but only marginally less tense, I went in to shower and dress, then called my best friend, Martha Harper, a detective for the Kings Harbor Police Department. She was an habitually early riser and was probably already at work. I wondered if she'd heard about Tommy. Although Kings Harbor was only a short fifteen minutes south of Cedar Hills, it was relatively sophisticated and news didn't travel nearly as fast there as it did in the tiny lakeside town nestled up against Rainbow Lake.

"Detective Harper," Martha's gravelly voice boomed.

"Hey. You hear about Tommy?"

"Had to read it in the paper. How come you didn't call me?"

"I was busy trying to figure out what happened. Anyway, I just called the hospital and he's still comatose. Booker's put a squelch on visitors, afraid that the perp might come back and try to finish the job."

"I don't get it, Cass. Why in the world would anyone want to hurt Tommy Green? I love that little munchkin." Every time Martha came to visit, Tommy insisted on chauffeuring her out to my place in his green speedboat and I expected he was enamored with her status as a cop.

"Me too, Mart. I don't know. But I'm working on it. Listen, you think you could call Maggie when you get a chance? She'd want to know."

"You sure you don't want to call her yourself?"

"I'd rather you did it, Martha. If you don't mind."

"Of course I don't. Listen, babe. I've got a meeting with the Captain that started five minutes ago, but call me if there's any change. Love you!" She hung up before I could even respond.

It was Monday morning and the local library wouldn't open until nine. That would give me plenty of time to swing by Tommy's and get a better look around, then maybe grab a little breakfast at the lodge. Booker usually stopped in for his breakfast around eight, and if I timed it right I might be able to find out what the crime scene had revealed. Erica had taken Tommy's books and papers with her when she left. Just another way to make me mad, I thought. With any luck, I could avoid Erica Trinidad all day.

Some of the people who lived on Rainbow Lake had road access, but I didn't mind having to go by boat. I gathered up my house trash, called the cats back in so they could nap away the day inside and jogged down the ramp to my boat. It was a blue seventeen-foot, open-bow Seaswirl that was just right for living on Rainbow Lake. I tossed the trash bag in back, warmed up the engine, then took off across the glassy lake, letting the morning chill revive my spirits. There is nothing quite as invigorating as skipping across water in a fast boat, and by the time I pulled up at the marina, I felt much better. But the absence of Tommy, who usually greeted me each morning, again dampened my spirits. Gus Townsend, who owned the marina, was pumping gas into a yellow bass boat.

"Understand you saw what happened," he said in his raspy smoker's voice. He had a craggy complexion and looked much older than his fifty-some-odd years. No matter how often he shaved, he always seemed to have a five-o'clock shadow. It looked to me like he'd been up all night at the tavern.

"Where the heck did you hear that?" I asked.

"Well, what I heard was that you and that niece of Walter Trinidad, the one who got himself killed a while back, were up in the restroom when it happened and saw the whole thing."

"You should know better than to believe half of what you hear in this town, Gus."

"Didn't say I believed it. Said I heard it. Anyway, them damn doctors won't even let me in to see how he's doing. I went over there last night and they said family only. Like I'm not practically family to the kid."

"Well, if it's any consolation, he probably wouldn't have known if you were there or not. He's still in a coma. What else are people saying? Any rumors about who might've done it?"

He threw back his head and laughed. "You askin' if there's rumors? Good God, girl. Ain't nothin' but. One story has it he was blackmailing some rich bastard on the lake. Another one has him diddlin' someone's wife and the husband didn't take too kindly to it. All sorts of speculation about who *that* might be. Quite a few candidates, if you know what I mean." He crinkled his eyes at me to let me know he was well aware of the extent of Tommy's sex life.

"What do *you* think?" I asked. He returned the gas nozzle to the pump and lit a cigarette, inhaling deeply.

"Well, I'll tell you what. Tommy has always been on time, never one to call in sick much. The last few weeks, he's been leavin' early, sneaking out at lunch, stuff like that. Didn't think I'd notice, maybe, 'cause I've been doin' construction out on the lake. But the wife notices from inside the shop and she tells me. Says a coupla times he got a ride with them Bailey boys, so I figure it isn't a girl problem. Maybe he's started doin' drugs. That Buck Bailey was always trouble. You can tell by them nose rings. Anyway, I figure maybe it was a drug deal gone bad. Maybe he owed somebody money, didn't pay up and they went after him."

It was as good a theory as any, I figured. I told Gus to take care and hauled my trash up the ramp to the dumpster, wondering how many people thought that Erica and I had seen what happened. I just hoped that whoever attacked Tommy didn't think so. Nothing worse than a bad guy thinking you're on to him when you're not.

I hopped into my Jeep Cherokee and headed for Tommy's, thinking about how to systematically go through his things and where to start. As it turned out, I needn't have bothered.

When I pulled up to his place, the first thing I noticed was Pepper curled up on the front porch in a patch of morning sun. Pepper should have been inside where Erica had left her.

I got out of the Jeep and walked quietly around the front of the mobile home. The window above the window box was shattered. Even from the porch, I could tell the place had been ransacked. Tommy's bed sheets were heaped on the floor, the clothes pulled out of his closet and flung haphazardly across the room. Books had been pulled from shelves and heaved across the room. Not only had someone gone through his things, but they'd done it angrily. I walked back to the garage and noticed the padlock had been cut with bolt cutters. Inside, tools had been pulled from shelves and boxes ripped open, their contents dumped on the concrete floor. I looked for the shovels that Tommy had supposedly borrowed but only saw one. Had the twins done this, then taken their shovels and left? Or had there never been any shovels to take? I knew Booker would have already checked the place. I wondered if he'd seen this mess, or if he'd stopped by before it had happened.

Suppressing my natural inclination to go inside, I went to the porch and picked up Pepper who seemed no worse for the wear.

"Bet you could tell me who did this, couldn't you? Was it those big bad Bailey brothers?" She started purring and showed me where to scratch under her chin. I thought about taking her back to my place, but she'd already survived the worst. What I needed to do was get Booker out here, if he hadn't already been, then clean the place up and get her back inside where I could make sure she had plenty of food, water and clean sand. That way, I'd have an excuse to come back out here and do my own snooping around. I doubted I'd find whatever someone had been looking for. They'd either found it themselves, or it hadn't been here in the first place. But I might discover more about what Tommy had been up to. First, though, I needed to make sure Booker had a chance to fingerprint the place. I knew if I screwed up the crime scene, he'd never forgive me. I set Pepper back on the porch and carefully retraced the steps to my Jeep, heading for the lodge to wait for Booker.

The lodge has two faces. At night, it's a top-notch restaurant with decent wines, a fairly upscale menu and a matching clientele. In the morning it's a haven for locals who want a good, cheap breakfast, heavy on cholesterol and served in Oregonian portions. Booker was there when I arrived, but to my dismay he was already having breakfast with his deputy, Newt

Hancock. I'd hoped to talk to him alone, without Deputy Do-little getting in the way. When Booker saw me, he waved me over and I pulled up a chair.

"You remember Newt," he said by way of introduction.

"Yes. Any news?" I smiled at New but directed my question to Booker. Newt looked half-asleep. He pushed his black Stetson up a fraction of an inch in greeting, peering at me from beneath those heavy lashes.

"Still in a coma. I've got it so family only can see him. Doctors agreed, which will make that part of our job easier. You get Erica home okay?" His blue eyes regarded me with interest. He was asking more than just after her welfare.

I said, "Didn't exactly see her to the door, but I assume she got there safe and sound," answering the question he really wanted to know without coming out and saying it. "Anything from the crime scene?"

Booker looked at Newt, then waved over the waitress. I watched the exchange, not sure how to read it. Newt's eyelashes lowered and he took another sip of his coffee.

"I know you're hungry," Booker said, winking at me. He waited until I'd ordered, then filled me in. "Nothing much to report. Found the weapon in the trashcan inside the restroom. It looks like the perp grabbed the metal pole that's used to open the bathroom window and hit Tommy from behind with it at least three times. The hook on the end's what did the damage, that and the location of the blows. Probably the only reason Tommy's still alive is that the pole broke in two. One more swing might've killed him."

"So you think Tommy was just a random target?"

Hancock spoke up in his lazy drawl. "Probably. They could've been waiting in the stall for someone to come along alone, then snuck up behind him, hit him over the head, grabbed the wallet and ran." He took another swallow of coffee and looked up at the waitress with the same bedroom eyes he'd tried on me yesterday.

"You got any cream for this, darlin'?"

"Got milk. That do ya?"

"Anything you bring'll do me just fine."

I rolled my eyes at Booker and dug into my scrambled eggs, wondering what Booker was keeping from me. It was obvious he wasn't going to divulge more with his deputy around.

"You been out to Tommy's place yet?" I asked, biting into my toast.

"Checked it out yesterday. Why?"

"Someone's been there since then. Tore up the place pretty bad."

Booker sat up and put his fork down. "When were you there?"

"Fifteen minutes ago. I went to feed the cat and found the place trashed. Didn't touch anything."

"You want me to go check it out?" Newt asked, pushing back his chair. He'd ordered pancakes and had devoured them in four bites.

"No. I want to see this for myself. You probably ought to finish that paperwork, then go see what the Lewis lady's going to do about those dogs."

Newt nodded, taking the menial assignments in stride. "I'll get started then," he said. "Good to see you again, Cassandra."

"You too, Nate." Two could play that game.

He did a slow double take and grinned. "Newt."

"Cassidy."

"Right." He dug a wad of bills from his wallet and laid them on the table, not bothering to count them out. "Breakfast's on me," he said. Booker and I watched him saunter out, his long legs crossing the room in slow motion, his alligator boots tapping the hardwood floor in a nice syncopated beat.

"You don't like him much, do you?" Booker asked, sorting through the money on the table.

"The guy's weird. Comes on to anything with two legs. And he looks like he's half-asleep all the time. I keep having to resist the urge to splash water in his face."

Booker chuckled. "He *could* use someone lightin' a fire underneath him. Complete opposite of his uncle, I'll tell you that. Don't think he really cares if he's a cop or not. Doing it for the prestige, I guess. His heart don't seem to be in it much. Maybe that's why his uncle sent him to me. Thought maybe I'd be the one to light that fire."

"Yeah, but your heart doesn't seem to be into training him much either. I get the feeling you don't think he *ought* to be a cop."

"Not for me to decide."

"So what else did you find at the scene?" I asked, changing the subject. Booker looked at me oddly.

"I saw the look you gave Newt, Tom. What gives?"

"Not much." He sighed and pushed his plate away, leaning back in his seat. "I should have secured the scene myself, that's all. I had no business going in the ambulance with Tommy. But I thought maybe he'd come to and I wanted to be there if he said something. I thought I could trust Newt to secure the scene until I returned."

"He didn't?"

"He found Tommy's wallet. It was stripped clean, of course. There's a nice piece of plastic where his driver's license goes. Good clean surface for prints."

"So? That's good, right?"

"Newt put his damn fingerprints all over the thing."

"Oh."

"Yeah. Now you know why I wasn't thrilled to send him over to Tommy's. Come on. I better get over there before someone else does and screws it up."

Booker had me wait outside at Tommy's. I stood in the doorway stroking Pepper and watched as he methodically went from room to room.

"What do you suppose they were looking for?" he asked, coming back out onto the porch. Guilt inched up my neck. I felt the heat and knew my cheeks were splotched red.

Oh, to hell with Erica, I thought. Booker was my friend, and he was Tommy's friend. "There's something I've been meaning to tell you," I said. Booker crossed his arms and listened while I told him what Tommy had said to Erica. Then I told him about our encounter with the Bailey brothers and about the books and maps Tommy had checked out from the library. Finally, I told him Tommy had downloaded information on obtaining a gun. The only thing I didn't mention was the flowers. I probably would have, but he cut me off.

"Why didn't you tell me this yesterday, Cass?"

I paused, not sure how to answer.

"You didn't think you could trust me?" He was incredulous.

"It's not that, Tom. It's just that Erica —"

"Erica. Right. Damn it all to hell, Cass. You shoulda told me straight off!" He was so mad, his naturally dark features looked sunburnt. Fuming, he paced the front porch. I waited until he calmed down, afraid that whatever I said would just make things worse. Finally, he stopped pacing and turned to face me.

"Well, seein' as you've had more time to mull this over than I have, you got any fancy ideas about what's goin' on?"

"Erica thinks that maybe Tommy found the other half of the clue and . . ."

He exploded. "I don't give a rat's ass what Erica Trinidad thinks. I want to know what you think!"

"Tom. I said I was sorry. I don't see what difference it makes whether I told you last night or this morning —"

He cut me off. "Well, I'll tell you. For one thing, if I'd known the Bailey brothers had been out here, I might've come out here myself and waited to see if they came back. Especially if I'd known that Tommy told Erica to find something. Someone emptied his wallet, Cass. Didn't just take the money. Took everything in it. Then someone came out here and went through the house like a tornado. They looked in the toilet tank, for God's sake. So whatever they were looking for wasn't real big. Small enough to fit in a wallet? I don't know. Now we don't even know if they found it or not. If I'd've known there was something to look for, I might've found it myself!"

I nodded, feeling genuinely terrible. "He also said

something about flowers," I said. "Just the word. It was the last thing he said."

Booker stared at me, his blue eyes steely. "You just now remembering this? You gonna remember something else in a minute or two? A day or week from now?"

"I swear to you, that's it. He said not to trust anyone, that Erica should find it, and then he said 'flowers' and passed out. I thought maybe we should check the flowerbed outside the restroom, but there were so many people there, looking and everything . . ."

"Jesus H. Christ!" he muttered. He strode off the porch like he was on his way to war, climbed into his cruiser, slammed the door and tore off, spraying pebbles and dirt in his wake.

"So much for honesty," I said, feeling like pond scum. I petted Pepper for a while to comfort myself, but she got tired of the attention and jumped down. Trying not to touch anything until Booker had a chance to print the place, I made sure Pepper had plenty of cat chow, then climbed back into my Jeep and headed back toward town, my mood about as low as it could get.

Chapter Six

The Cedar Hills Library was in an old brick building dating back to the days when the town was a thriving logging village. The little old lady who ran the place was almost as old as the building. Mrs. Peters had white hair that often took on pink or bluish tints, depending on which brand of rinse she was using at the time. She wore a pink sweater buttoned at the top and open at the waist to allow room for her generous midsection. When she saw me, her watery eyes lit up. She wore trifocals and her eyes always seemed huge behind them.

"Cassidy James! One of my favorite bookworms!"

See? I thought. *Some*one likes me!

"Hey, Mrs. Peters. How you doing?"

"I'm fair, Cassidy. Just fair. Poor, poor Tommy Green. Such a shame. I had a cousin once, went into a coma. Lasted more than a year before they decided to pull the plug. I hope they don't do that with Tommy — leave him hanging on. I'm a firm believer that when it's your time, it's your time. None of that artificial resuscitation nonsense for me. What can I do for you?"

"Actually, it's Tommy I came to see you about. You remember him checking out some books a while back?"

"Sure do. They're overdue, too. The lost treasure stuff has been a real popular subject lately. Kind of goes in waves over the years. There'll be an article or something in the paper about that old lost gold and all of a sudden people start checking out books on it, wanting to know everything they can on the subject. I even showed Tommy and his friend how to use the microfiche and he photocopied some old news articles on it."

"What friend was that?"

"Oh, I wouldn't know that. A red-headed boy. Kind of dirty-looking."

Bart Bailey. "Did you happen to read or see whatever it was that got him interested in the first place?"

"No-o-o." She put her finger to her temple. "Thinking back, I have to assume there was something, because of all the sudden interest."

"So he wasn't the only one checking out books about the lost gold?"

"No. A couple of others did too, right about the same time."

"You remember who?"

"I remember one of them. Just a minute." She went back behind the oak counter and hit buttons on her computer.

It always amazed me to see older people using the latest technology like they'd done it all their lives. She was easily an octogenarian, yet could talk RAM, gigabytes and megahertz with the best of them.

"Well, I guess the one I remember didn't actually check anything out or I'd have it on file. I do recall he sat right over there and pored through half a dozen stories on that old lost treasure though. Seemed odd to me, because he looked more the type to be reading Shakespeare, not old folklore."

"You remember what he looked like?"

"Oh, I certainly do. He was in his late sixties and I'd never seen him before, which was why I noticed. Most of the older folks around here I know. He had white hair, kind of longish, with a moustache and beard to match. Sort of reminded me of a more refined Grandpa Walton. I figured him to be a new retiree out on the lake. I ruled out the mobile home park because his sweater was a cardigan and his loafers were real leather. A retired doctor maybe. Anyway, I was surprised that the only thing he seemed interested in were the stories on the lost treasure. It didn't fit with who I had him pegged for."

"And this was before or after Tommy checked out his books?"

"Oh, before, I'm fairly sure. Yes, it was. Because when Tommy started asking for the same kind of materials, I thought, 'Aha! There's been another documentary on that old logger who supposedly found half a note telling where the gold was hidden.' Like I said, over the years, I've seen it happen before."

"You said someone else was interested in the gold about that time?"

"Yes, I've got that one here. A Ginny Cathwaite. Hadn't seen her in here before either. She just checked out the one book."

"When was that?"

"Let's see. Just a day after Tommy checked out his. I only carry the two copies and they were both checked out. I can go a whole year without either one being so much as looked at."

"Did she return her book?"

"Oh, yes. Only kept it a day or two. I've got it here, if you'd like to take a look at it." She led me to the shelf and I recognized the book as a copy of the one I'd seen the night before. I flipped through the well-worn pages, stopping to glance again at the picture of the half-torn note the logger had found. The page was dog-eared, like over the years readers had zeroed in on this one page.

"You want to check it out?" she asked.

"No, thanks. I know you wouldn't normally do this, but would you give me a call if someone else comes in asking for it?"

Mrs. Peters narrowed her eyes at me and pushed her glasses up on the bridge of her nose. "This have something to do with what happened to Tommy?"

"I'm not sure," I said truthfully. "I'm just sort of looking at all the angles. You remember what this Ginny Cathwaite looked like?"

"Little bitty thing, as I recall. Reminded me of a cheerleader, though she must've been in her forties.

Seemed to know just what she was looking for. Afraid I can't recall much more. I believe I was working on the computer when she came in." She looked down, as if admitting an embarrassing addiction.

"You still surfing the Net?" I asked. Since the advent of the Internet, Mrs. Peters had been a voracious e-mailer, chat-room lobbyist and all around Web browser. She was as addicted to the Net as a gambler to a slot machine.

She looked at me, her watery eyes revealing both pride and chagrin. "I have a pen pal in Pakistan, of all places. Can you believe it? You wouldn't believe the things that women put up with back there."

"Did you by any chance show Tommy how to download information? I found something at his house that looks like it came from a Web site and Tommy doesn't even own a computer."

"Yes, as a matter of fact, I did. He came in last week and I reminded him that his books were overdue. He said he'd get them back to me directly and could I show him how to buy something off the computer. He wouldn't tell me what he was interested in, so I gave him the basics and let him browse on his own. He was here quite a while but I don't know if he found what he was looking for. He did print something, though, so maybe he was successful." She looked over at her computer fondly, as if anxious to get back in front of it, so I thanked her for her help and walked outside into what had become another bright, sunshine-filled day.

The library was only a few blocks from the county park and I decided to walk over, half-hoping I'd run into Booker, half-afraid to. Apparently, he'd already been and gone. The flowerbeds looked fairly well-trampled and the crime-scene tape had been extended to wrap around their perimeter. Had he found something? The county park workers were out in numbers, cleaning up after the festival. Despite the attack on Tommy, the festivities had gone on, and from the looks of the grounds, been a smashing success. Idly, I wondered who'd won the chowder contest. It seemed a lifetime since I'd stood just a hundred feet away, tasting chowders while half the town looked on. Had whoever attacked Tommy been watching the contest too? Or had he —presuming it was a man who attacked him in the restroom — been watching Tommy, waiting for him to break away from the crowd so he could approach him?

And why attack him in such a public place? Why not just wait until he got home, then sneak up on him there? Was it because the assailant thought that Tommy had whatever it was he wanted *on* him? I shook my head, knowing I had more questions than answers. It was time to talk to someone who could answer some of them.

Bart Bailey worked at an auto repair shop just outside of Cedar Hills on Highway One. He specialized in broken-down motor homes and big rigs, but I'd seen him work on Tommy's boat once, so I knew his mechanic's skills were diverse. When I pulled into the parking lot, he was bent over the engine of a station wagon, doing something with a wrench.

"Got a minute?" I asked, startling him. He banged his head on the hood and stood up, rubbing at the spot.

"Uh, sure," he said. "It's kind of slow right now, anyway. It's Cass, right?" Up close, Bart was an interesting study in hues, and though not exactly handsome, his features were pleasing. His intelligent green eyes were ringed with pale lashes and his cheeks were blotched with color as if he'd just exercised. The smattering of freckles splashed across his nose were tarnished copper and added to the Tom Sawyer look. He wore his frizzy red hair tied back in a ponytail, but tendrils had broken loose and strayed down along the darker auburn sideburns. Pushed back from his high forehead, he wore a grease-stained Yankees cap that had seen better days.

"How come you trashed Tommy's place, Bart?"

His eyes widened, then he shook his head. "No way. Not me. If his place got trashed, it wasn't my doing. You can ask anyone. I was at the tavern until closing time. Then I left with Candy Morris." He spoke rapidly, breathing shallowly.

"Didn't say when it happened, Bart, but you seem to have a pretty good idea. What time did Buck leave the bar?"

"Why don't you ask him?" There was a hint of defiance, but his eyes didn't back it up. He seemed to realize he wasn't going to pull off a tough-guy act. His shoulders slumped and he let out a gargantuan sigh.

" 'Cause I wanted to hear what you had to say first, Bart. What were you guys looking for?"

"I wasn't there!" His voice rose. He looked around as if embarrassed by his outburst, then lowered his voice. "I told you. It wasn't me."

"Okay, okay. I believe you. What was Buck looking for?"

He shook his head. Shrugged. Looked at me with obvious anxiety.

"I know about the gold thing, Bart. About the hidden treasure you and Tommy were looking for. Was Buck in on it, too?"

His eyes went wide. He looked like a precocious twelve-year-old. "How'd you know that?"

"You guys weren't exactly discreet. You checked out books from the library. Tommy started missing work. You three were seen hanging out together. I know you guys were up there on Rainbow Ridge looking for the treasure. What I don't understand is what Tommy had that Buck wanted so badly."

"You're a private detective, right? Tommy told me. Said you were a, uh . . ." He paused, his cheeks turning pink. "You know. Like Ellen."

"Ellen?"

"On TV. You know." Bart was definitely blushing.

"A bookstore owner?"

Bart's gaze met mine and he smiled at his own expense. "Sorry. You must think I'm a total moron. I sound like an idiot."

"It's okay, Bart. The word's *lesbian*."

"Right." His face was beet red. "Anyway, Tommy said you're good people. Said you were someone he could talk to. If Tommy trusted you, I guess I can too." Bart took a breath and looked over his shoulder as if afraid someone would see us talking. Someone like Buck, probably.

"Come on, Bart. Let me buy you a soda."

There was a truckstop next to the repair shop. The waitress seemed to know Bart and greeted him warmly. Bart had a shy smile. He used it sparingly, but when he smiled, he was actually cute. We slid into a booth and ordered Cokes. As soon as the waitress left, Bart removed his cap, smoothed his red hair and leaned forward, his eyes locked on mine.

"Buck didn't attack Tommy, if that's what you're thinking. I knew someone would think that and I told him to just leave Tommy's place alone, but Buck gets an idea in his head and he can't get it out."

"So why did he trash the place? What was he looking for?"

"It's kind of complicated." He took a deep breath. "You already know about the lost gold, right? I'd never even heard of it myself, until one night at the bar when this old guy comes in and starts moaning about how he was this close to being rich and now he's up and got some weird disease and what a waste of good fortune. Anyway, Tommy buys him a few drinks and the next thing you know he's telling us the story about this gold hidden somewhere up on Rainbow Ridge and how he's found the other half of this note that's supposed to tell where the gold is hidden, only he can't reach it because the trees have grown so tall and now, being terminal with no relatives, what's the point anyway, and like that. So Buckie starts buying him more drinks and before the night is over, he's told us exactly where the tree is that's got the pouch that's got the note supposedly tied to some red bandana. He even drew us a map on a napkin. You know, I only half-believed the old guy, but Tommy and Buck were completely sold on it, and the next morning they were already making plans on what to do with the money."

Our Cokes came and Bart practically drained his in one slurp through the straw. Talking seemed to be doing him some good, and he sat back in the booth, more relaxed.

"It started out the three of us, even-steven partners. Whichever one of us found the red bandana first, we'd tell the others, right? The plan was, we'd go up to where the guy had told us and start searching the trees for the bandana. Buck got ahold of some tree-climbing equipment — boots with spikes on 'em, special belts with pulleys, ropes, binoculars, stuff like that. I mean, we had some money invested in this venture. Well, actually, it was my money and Tommy's. But Buck did the legwork, had the connections and stuff. Anyway, we started going up every chance we got, but both Tommy and I had to work and couldn't go as often as Buck wanted. Buck said he'd go by himself, if it was all right with us, but Tommy insisted that none of us go without the other two. Buck seemed okay with that and never mentioned it again."

He finished the Coke and leaned forward, resting his grease-stained elbows on the table. I waited for him to go on.

"Then, last week, Tommy comes to me and says Buck's holding out on us. Says he has proof that Buck has found the clue and that he's working with someone else. I told him no way Buck would do that to me but Tommy's like all agitated and says he can prove it. So I say, how, and he says he followed Buck and got a picture of his truck and also another car which proved that Buck was working with someone else. He said he followed Buck up the trail and found his backpack and climbing gear and decided to look through the pack. Inside was the clue we'd been looking for. Tommy says he took the note and hid it because for one, he wanted to prove to me that my brother was cheating us and two, he figured the note was ours as much as Buck's." He paused, looking around for the waitress.

"Did he show you the note?"

"He was going to, but then he got mad and accused me of being in on it with Buck. See, I didn't want to believe Tommy. I mean, Buck's different, you know, but he's still my brother. People think he's just a dumb jock, but actually he's pretty smart. But it's like he doesn't want people to know he's smart, so he acts dumb, gets into fights a lot and can be mean, especially to my friends. That's why I figured he was pulling a prank on Tommy." Bart's green eyes were watching me closely.

"I don't get it," I said.

He sighed. "Every friendship I ever had, I mean with a good friend, Buck figured out a way to screw it up. I figured this was just another example of Buck trying to get between me and a friend." Bart smiled at the waitress, who brought him another Coke without asking, then returned his gaze to me.

"So you thought he was playing a prank?"

"Exactly. I figured Tommy wouldn't lie to me, so the only explanation had to be that Buck knew Tommy was checking up on him and decided to plant a phony note, just to freak Tommy out. I guess you'd have to know Buck to understand this, but trust me, it's something he would do. Anyway, I confronted Buck myself, told him that Tommy had followed him to the ridge, taken pictures of his truck and another car and had found the phony note in his backpack. I told him to admit that he'd tried to fool Tommy with a phony note. I said I knew for a fact that it was phony, 'cause I had found the real one myself."

"Whoa. Back up a second. You found a note, too?"

Bart smiled sheepishly, toying with his glass. "I told you this was complicated. See, after Tommy told me that Buck was up there working on his own, I followed him myself, just to see."

"When was this?" I interrupted.

"Friday. I took the afternoon off and went looking for Buck. He was parked at the bottom of the ridge all right, so I started up after him, then decided it would be interesting just to watch him through the binoculars from this granite ledge I'd seen. Easier than tracking him, too. Anyway, I got up there and started searching the trees and ground and all of the sudden I saw the red bandana myself about two thirds the way up this humongous fir tree! I couldn't believe it! First of all, I was relieved that Tommy was wrong about Buck. Then I started getting all sweaty and my heart started pounding hard because I realized I'd found the real clue!"

"And?" I hated to say so, but the chance of even one bandana staying tied to a tree for a hundred years and somehow maintaining its red color seemed pretty remote. I bit my tongue and let him continue.

"I picked out a landmark, counted trees and tried to memorize where it was. Seeing it from the ledge was one thing. Finding it from the bottom would be something else. Anyway, I figured it was going to take at least two of us to get to it, maybe using walkie-talkies with the person on the ledge giving directions. I was so excited, I couldn't think straight. Now that I'd found the real clue, I didn't even care about

Buckie's little game. But when I got back to town and told Tommy, he started accusing me of being part of Buck's plan, trying to throw him off-track. As soon as he got the film developed he was gonna prove that Buck was cheating us. I told him that maybe Buck *was* up there looking, but that the note was a phony, just to fool Tommy. But Tommy wasn't buying it. He said he'd checked and the note he had taken from Buck's backpack was real. Then he started looking at me like I was in on it with Buck and he just stormed away."

Bart leaned back and blew red wisps off his forehead, clearly upset by what had happened. But at the same time, he seemed relieved to be sharing it with someone.

"I called him Saturday night after he'd calmed down a little, and that's when he said that he'd show me the pictures and note the next day. Then Buck comes in demanding to know what Tommy and I were discussing and I just flat out told him everything — how Tommy had seen his truck and followed him, how he'd found the phony note in Buck's pack, how I'd known all along that it was just a prank, and how I had seen the real bandana from up on the ledge. Well, instead of being excited about what I'd found, Buck went ballistic. Said he was gonna kill that sorry little punk, and that if I knew what was good for me I'd steer clear. I know that sounds pretty incriminating but, the thing is, you have to know Buck. He says stuff like that all the time, doesn't mean anything. But the way he reacted, I started thinking that maybe he wasn't just playing a prank. Maybe Tommy was right about him cheating us. But then, what about the bandana I saw in the tree?"

"And this was Saturday night?"

"Yeah. I know what you're thinking. That Buck's the one who jumped Tommy in the park the next day, but he's not. He was mad and he wanted his note back, but I know he wouldn't have actually hurt Tommy. I think he did go to the park to confront him but by then it was too late. Someone else had gotten to him."

"How about this other car? Buck say who was with him?"

Bart shook his head, his green eyes puzzled. "He had no idea what Tommy was talking about, and I believe him on that. What's the point in lying? Yesterday he admitted to me that he'd kept the note to himself because he didn't trust Tommy. He swears he was going to tell me once the time was right. Now all he wants is to find the note again. I told him to leave Tommy's place alone, but I just knew he wouldn't listen."

"You really think your brother found a note that no one else has been able to find all these years?"

"Well, he and Tommy both think so. But what about the bandana I saw?"

"Anyone else know about all this?"

"Not as far as I know. Except maybe whoever was in the other car Tommy saw. Maybe if you find him, you'll know what happened to Tommy."

Which was exactly what I'd been thinking.

"So you don't know if Buck found what he was looking for at Tommy's last night or not?"

"I kind of doubt it."

"Why's that?"

"When I got home this morning, he was passed out on the sofa, and from the look of things, I could tell he'd really tied one on. Buck only does that when he's really, really ticked off. He wasn't celebrating, Cass. He was working himself into a rage."

Chapter Seven

After talking to Bart, I headed straight for the little clapboard duplex he shared with his brother, but Buck was already gone. According to Bart, Buck only worked odd jobs and wasn't currently employed. Chances were, he was up on Rainbow Ridge in search of the lost treasure. If I wanted to talk to him, I'd probably have to find him there, but I wasn't exactly prepared for a hike in the wilderness just then. On the other hand, there was nothing that said I couldn't poke around a little, just to get a feel for the guy.

Well, there was the law against breaking and entering, of course, but I try not to dwell on the little stuff.

Their unit was in back, off the street and away from prying eyes. As I passed the front unit, a small dog barked but nobody peered out the window, so I was fairly certain no one was home. I knocked on their door again, making sure they didn't have a dog, then took out my picks. It only took me a minute to spring the cheap lock and I was inside.

Where Tommy's place had been relatively neat and homey, Buck and Bart lived in disarray. Right away I could tell that one of them was a slob, and it didn't take long to figure out which one. While the kitchen was neat enough, the living room was strewn with both under- and outer-garments in serious need of laundering. A note on the refrigerator door reminded Buck it was his turn to take out the trash, but when I checked under the sink, it was obvious he'd ignored the reminder. The bathroom sink had been recently cleaned, but the toilet was unflushed. One bedroom showed a neatly made bed and organized closet; the other was a disaster area. Buck's room smelled of bourbon and cigarettes, and a few of the beer cans he used for ashtrays had toppled over, spilling a sooty fluid onto the cheap laminate desktop.

How in the world did twins end up like Oscar Madison and Felix Unger? I wondered. Was Bart driven to clean up Buck's messes because of some innate sense of order? Or was Buck reckless and disorderly out of rebellion against Bart's orderly nature? The poor mother, I thought. On the other hand, it could've been worse. She could've had two like Buck.

Gingerly, without wanting to breathe in the rancid odors of Buck's closet, I went through his pants' pockets, finding matches, a stick of gum, a crumpled dollar bill, but nothing of importance. If he'd found what he was looking for at Tommy's, he'd probably taken it with him. Still, I crawled under the bed, searching for any clue that might shed some light on whether Buck had been the one to attack Tommy. Unless soiled socks and a moldy potato chip were evidence, it was a wasted effort.

Next, I went through Buck's drawers and was rewarded with equally worthless findings. But in the top drawer, beneath the wadded-up boxer shorts and white T-shirts, I unearthed a framed photograph of the Bailey brothers, around age seven, with their parents and little sister. The mother, a redhead like the boys, had a sweet smile, reminding me of Bart. She had her hands on both boys' shoulders and was gazing fondly at Bart, who was grinning gap-toothed at his brother. The father was a burly man with a Marine-style crew cut and smile that leaned toward a smirk. His arms were crossed, showing bulging biceps and what looked like well-practiced impatience. But what I found most interesting was Buck. The meanness hadn't crept into his eyes yet and his smile seemed genuine. He held his little redheaded sister in his arms with obvious adoration. She looked like a miniature Shirley Temple, all dimples and curls. It was a revealing snapshot, I thought. The mother adored Bart. Bart adored Buck, Buck adored the sister, and the father adored no one except maybe himself. But how had that angelic boy turned into such a hardened bully? When had his sweet nature turned into anger? And anger at whom? What had happened to Buck Bailey that made him so unlikable?

I stuffed the photo back down into the drawer and

moved to the desk, avoiding the gunk that had seeped out of the spilled beer cans. A desk lamp had been left on and beneath it was a phone book opened to the T's. Idly, I scanned the page, wondering who Buck had wanted to call. I pushed redial on the phone and listened with disappointment to the spiel from Dominick's Pizza Pub. Obviously, that wasn't the number Buck had sought. Or maybe it wasn't a phone number he wanted at all, but rather an address. I continued down the page and was almost to the bottom when the name jumped out at me, making my pulse quicken. E. Trinidad on Willow Cove in Cedar Hills. Erica's address. Why would Buck Bailey be interested in where Erica Trinidad lived? Did he suspect that she knew more than she'd said?

I finished my search hastily, knowing I'd already stayed inside longer than I should have. It was mid-afternoon and I still needed to check on Tommy. Maybe he'd come to and could clear everything up, I thought optimistically. I kept that hope alive on the drive to the hospital, but only made it as far as the nurse's station before being stopped by a white-garbed gendarme in a sour mood. I explained who I was, but her lips were pursed and she was shaking her head and there was no way I was going to get past her. She assured me that his condition was unchanged, that my number was on the list to call if something did change, and that meanwhile his mother, sister and aunt were visiting as often as allowed.

"Do you know where I might find them?" I tried, knowing Tommy didn't have a sister. Maybe a girlfriend was posing as a sister, so she could get in to see him, I thought.

"I believe the sheriff took them to lunch. They

seem to be holding up just fine." In other words, I should butt out.

I stopped at MacGregors on the way back and shopped for groceries. Whenever I'm upset, I cook, and with everything that had happened the past two days, I was in need of some serious culinary therapy. I picked up some chanterelles, a pint of half-and-half, a pound of butter, some Parmisiano Reggiano, an artichoke, some chicken breasts and a few other odds and ends I didn't have on hand. Then I sped back to my place, letting the summer sunshine soothe my soul and the cool breeze lift my spirits.

To my surprise, when I rounded the island, I could see someone standing on my dock, waving something in the air. Was someone in trouble? My pulse quickened and my mind raced with possibilities. As I drew closer, however, I saw it was a white flag being waved and the person doing the waving was Erica Trinidad. She wasn't in trouble. She was calling for a truce.

"Cute," I said, suppressing a smile as I pulled up to the dock. Erica bent over and secured the lines to metal cleats. She was wearing white cotton shorts that showed off long brown legs and a tank top that showed off the rest of her. Her dark hair was damp and unbrushed, as if she'd just been for a swim and hadn't completely dried off. I handed her a bag of groceries and climbed out with the other two. "Where's your boat?"

"I hid it around the cove in that willow brush. It took me fifteen minutes to walk a few hundred yards of shoreline, can you believe it? I had to jump in the lake to cool off."

"Why'd you hide your boat, Erica?"

"I think someone's been following me. I think there were two people in the boat, but I can't be positive. I noticed them just outside the marina. They stayed back, but kept making the same turns I was. When I pulled into my place, they went on past, but I'd swear they were tailing me. I waited until I couldn't see them anymore, then came over here and hid the boat. I saw them go by real slowly a little while ago but they never turned into this cove."

Buck Bailey had looked up Erica's address. Was he following her? If so, why? And who was with him? I wondered if he owned a boat. Maybe he'd had to borrow a friend's.

"What kind of boat?"

"A little bigger than yours, but flatter, like a ski boat. Dark-colored, I think. They never got close enough for me to see more." She paused and waited for me to look at her. "Cass, about last night. I'm sorry. I was out of line and acted like a jerk."

"Right on both counts. Come on. You can help me put these away, then put something warmer on. You look cold."

Erica looked down at her chest and I could've sworn she blushed. "I was going to call you later, let you know how Tommy was . . ." she said.

"You got in to see Tommy?" I wheeled around, staring incredulously.

She grinned. "I said I was his sister. I met his mom and aunt and they vouched for me. They're really nice. Tommy probably didn't know we were there, of course. You should see him, Cass. He looks smaller. All these tubes and monitors. It's scary. Anyway, Booker took us to lunch and I got to know them pretty well. You can see why Tommy's such a nice guy."

"How did Booker seem?" I asked.

"Charming as usual, in front of the others. He sure let me have an earful though, when he walked me to my car."

"I had to tell him, Erica. It was wrong not to tell him sooner."

She nodded and followed me up the walkway to the house. Panic and Gammon greeted us vociferously, rubbing our ankles and making our path to the kitchen more difficult.

"What are you going to make?" Erica asked, unpacking groceries. She threw an empty sack on the floor and Panic dove into it, her long twitching tail the only part sticking out. Gammon, all twenty pounds of her, pounced on the sack and a hilarious battle ensued.

"I was in the mood for pasta. Thought I'd saute the chanterelles, then make a Parmesan cream sauce, grill the chicken, steam the artichoke, like that."

"If I promise to do all the dishes, feed the cats and never argue with you again, will you invite me to stay for dinner?"

"Only if you help with the pasta. You can start by getting the machine down."

"Deal." She was leaning against the kitchen table, watching me sort through the refrigerator. "God, I've missed you, Cass."

I turned around, dumbstruck.

"I'm not going to come on to you, I promise. I just wanted you to know. I won't say it again."

I turned back to the refrigerator, unsure what I'd

been looking for. My face felt flushed. Damn her, anyway. I finally pulled out some olive oil to make a marinade for the chicken, then went out to the greenhouse to pick some fresh basil. By the time I came back in, I was more composed.

Erica minced garlic while I set up the pasta machine. While we worked, I told her about Tommy's place being trashed and my talks with the librarian and Bart Bailey. She was a good listener and didn't miss much.

"Kind of funny how no one finds this clue for more than a hundred years, then the Bailey brothers suddenly find two of them."

"I know. Maybe Buck did make a phony clue to throw Tommy and Bart off-track, only it wasn't the one Tommy got, but the one Bart saw in the tree. I don't know. The whole thing seems silly. I mean, let's say for a second that there *is* a bandana. After a hundred years in the elements, there wouldn't be anything left! It certainly wouldn't still be red. Would it?"

"I don't know. How about the old man that told them about the gold in the first place? Doesn't that seem a little weird?"

"To say the least. Maybe Mrs. Peters was right about there having been some kind of documentary on the lost gold. Maybe the old guy in the bar had seen it too and was just pulling the guys' legs. You want a glass of wine?"

"You sure you trust me with it?"

Actually, I wasn't. But Erica had never needed alcohol to speak her mind. She did it stone cold sober, too. I rolled my eyes at her and pointed toward the wine cellar. "And put on something warmer. Grab a sweatshirt or something!" Erica giggled, but marched obediently into my bedroom, emerging in an old flannel shirt and a pair of thin cotton sweatpants. It felt odd, seeing her in my clothes. She ducked into the wine room, where she spent a long time going through the racks. When she came out, she held a Pinot Gris aloft as if she'd found hidden treasure herself. She uncorked the bottle and poured two glasses, breathing in the heady aromas before tasting.

"You ready to make pasta?" I asked. "Or are you just going to stand there with your nose in that glass all night?"

She took another slow sip, then took an apron from a hook on the wall and slipped it over her head, tying it behind her. "At your service, Madam Pasta Queen. Tell me what to do."

"Eggs," I said.

Erica curtsied and opened the refrigerator, producing the egg carton with a flourish.

"Flour," I said.

Erica whirled around, doing a rather sexy version of a pirouette, and retrieved the flour bin. "Flour," she repeated, handing it to me. Suddenly she looked stricken. "Oh, my God. I never thought of that."

"What?"

"Flour. Maybe he said 'flour.' "

"Tommy?"

"I mean, I heard *flowers*. Or *flower*. But maybe it was *flour*."

"I'm pretty sure it was plural when you first told me," I said, feeling my stomach tighten.

"Well, maybe I was wrong!"

Without saying another word, I turned off the burner, put the marinating chicken breasts back in the fridge and raced Erica for the boat.

At first glance, Tommy's place looked no worse than when Booker and I had left it, which was to say it looked terrible. Pepper complained loudly when we entered and led us directly to the kitchen where her food bowl was nearly empty which surprised me. I'd filled it with enough food for days. A second glance told me the reason — the bowl had been tipped and the crunchies were scattered across the kitchen floor. Maybe someone else had paid a visit after Booker and I left. Had whoever it was also searched through the rubble, looking for something?

I looked around the kitchen at the newly created mess. The table and chairs had been upended. The drawers were pulled open, and in some cases, their meager contents dumped on the counter. Tommy's kitchen wasn't particularly well-equipped, but it was clear that he did some cooking. He even had an old Betty Crocker cookbook that had been thrown unceremoniously with a few other books on the floor. I held my breath and opened a cupboard, looking for a flour bin. No luck. I opened the pantry cupboard and found, amid the jars of salsa and cans of chili beans, right next to a box of brown sugar, a blue and white sack of flour. My heart skipped a beat.

Hoping against hope, I dug down into the cool soft fluff and felt around. My fingers brushed against a sharper object and my heart skipped another beat, maybe two. Carefully, I pulled out a small plastic, resealable freezer Baggie. Inside were several photos and an ancient-looking scrap of paper. Quickly, I slid the Baggie into my jacket pocket and headed for the door.

"Let's get out of here!"

"I'm bringing Pepper. This place gives me the creeps!" Erica bundled Pepper in her arms and raced out behind me to the Jeep.

Chapter Eight

We went to Erica's first to retrieve Tommy's book and she asked me if I minded her packing a few items into an overnight bag. I hadn't actually invited her to stay and I wasn't sure how I felt about it. But I had plenty of extra room and as long as she stayed in the guest bedroom with Pepper, I supposed it was all right. Until we found out who was following her and why, it was probably a good idea for us to lay low.

I suspected that Panic and Gammon would be less than thrilled to meet Pepper, and I was right. Panic hissed and made herself twice her height, showing off her tail. Gammon took a few sniffs, turned up her nose and stomped off to guard her food dish. For her part, Pepper held her own, showing Panic her own tail and making her orange fluff puff out in all directions. Erica lifted Pepper, cooing softly and carried her into the guest room, losing major points with Panic. While they got settled into their new digs, I comforted both my cats, gave them a few kitty treats, then went out to light the barbecue. As anxious as I was to look at what Tommy had hidden, food and comfort came first.

Only after the pasta was made and hanging on dowels, the sauce simmering, the artichoke steaming and the coals burning down to a fine white ash did Erica and I sit down with our wine and examine the contents of the Baggie.

"Recognize this one?" I asked, pointing to the first picture.

"Buck Bailey's truck," Erica said. "But whose car is this?" she said, picking up the second photograph.

"No idea. Look. He got a good shot of the plate. I wonder if Tommy found out who it belonged to." The vehicle in question was an older model black Explorer with Oregon plates. The back of Buck's truck was just visible, parked a hundred feet or so up the narrow, rutted dirt road. "Buck might not have even known this car was here," I said, "if they came after he arrived and left before he did. Bart thought Buck was telling the truth. Who knows? Maybe he was."

"Maybe someone else overheard the old guy in the bar that night and was following Buck?"

"Maybe." I carefully eased out the last item, a worn and faded piece of brown parchment with jagged edges, torn down the middle.

Erica opened the book to the page where the old-timer's note had been copied and held Tommy's note up beside it.

"I'll be damned," she said. Suddenly, the sentences were complete, with a few exceptions where the paper was worn through. What remained was a detailed explanation of where the treasure was hidden. "You think it's real?"

"Hell, Erica. We don't even know if the one in the book's real. 'Bout-a-mile Bob could've been pulling everyone's leg. Maybe Bart was right and Buck was pulling Tommy's leg. Or like I said earlier, the old man in the bar might have been putting one over on the boys." I picked up the torn parchment and held it to the light. "Maybe we can get this age-tested."

"It does look like they match pretty well. But if this one's real, what about the bandana Bart saw?"

I held the two up closer, then started looking at individual letters and the way certain letter-pairs connected. About halfway down the page, I spotted a discrepancy. "See this *g*? The little fishhook loop at the end? The one in the book isn't like that."

Erica studied the letters, frowning. "I bet if you checked my writing, you'd find mismatches, too."

"Here's another one. See how the crossbar on this *T* is heavier than on the stem? The ones in the book aren't like that. Someone faked this letter, Erica. I'd bet on it. Wait a second, I want to check something out."

I went into my study and searched the bookshelves until I found what I was looking for.

"What's that?" she asked when I came back into the room.

"A manual on handwriting analysis. I used it a couple of years ago when I suspected that a husband had faked his wife's suicide note. It's an inexact science, but some amateur psychologists swear by it and it can be pretty revealing in terms of personality traits. Anyway, I know there's something in here on heavy crossbars." I flipped through the pages until I found the right section. "Here it is," I said. "I knew heavy crossbars were bad news. According to this, whoever forged the note is probably domineering and insensitive. They say a heavy cross bar is a distinctive abnormality and a fairly reliable indicator of an overbearing personality."

"Sounds like Buck to *me*."

"Yeah. But it sure seems like a lot of work for Buck to go to when he's in the middle of hunting for treasure."

I took a sip of wine, wondering if I should call Booker and ask him to run the plate for me, or whether I should just ask Martha. Booker wasn't the type to hold a grudge, but on the other hand, I'd never seen him so angry, at least not with me. Maybe I should give him a day or two to cool down, I thought. So I called Martha.

I caught her at the office working late, and when she heard my voice, she became somber.

"Something happen with Tommy?"

I assured her he was the same, then told her about the lost treasure and the car Tommy had seen up on Rainbow Ridge. "I was wondering if you'd run the license plate for me?"

"Hit me," she said.

I gave her the number, thinking she'd probably just jot it down and get back to me later. To my surprise, she punched in the numbers right then and told me to wait. I could hear her moving around her office, banging file drawers, and I felt guilty for bothering her at work. But when she came back on, she sounded almost cheerful.

"Well, that was easy. Looks like you're barking up the wrong tree, though. Plate belongs to a cop."

"You're kidding? Can you tell me who?"

"Sure. You probably know him. Tom Booker's new deputy, Newt Hancock."

Erica had started banging pots in the background and I carried the walk-around phone outside but not before Martha heard the clatter. "You got company?"

"Uh, sort of." I'd skipped the part about Erica Trinidad in my recounting of Tommy's attack, but now I was forced to tell her. As I expected, Martha started to chortle. "What?" I asked.

"You know damn well what. She doing the dishes, or just rearranging the furniture?"

"Very funny, Mart. She's here because she thinks someone was following her and after what happened to Tommy, we're being cautious."

"Uh-huh." I knew that sound. Martha was on the brink of laughter, barely containing her glee. "She gonna spend the night?"

"Martha!"

"Well?"

"If she does," I said, practically whispering as I walked farther out onto the deck, "it will be in the guest room."

"Uh-huh," she murmured again. "Listen, girlfriend. I really do have to run, but I want to hear every sordid detail, and soon!"

Somehow, I knew she wasn't talking about what had happened to Tommy. We made a lunch date for Wednesday, then I went inside to tell Erica the news.

"You won't believe this," I said. "The Explorer belongs to Newt Hancock. You think he was following Buck for some reason?"

"I don't know. Wish I'd known sooner. I could've asked him today. I think the guy is hitting on me."

"You saw Hancock again today?"

"Yeah. He was at the marina when I got back from the hospital. Even walked me down to my boat. He was very solicitous, asking about Tommy and all, but I think he was more interested in me, if you know what I mean."

I knew exactly what she meant. I'd seen Hancock's bedroom eyes in action myself. Erica's, too, for that matter. Of the two, Hancock's didn't hold a candle.

We swapped theories and speculations all through dinner and late into the night. Erica kept her promise, doing the dishes and refraining from making any advances. Panic finally couldn't stand it anymore and went to bat paws with Pepper beneath the guest bedroom door. Gammon burrowed herself into my lap, letting me know just who belonged to who. All in all, it was a perfectly lovely evening. I went to bed feeling strangely buoyant, and it had nothing at all to do with the wine.

Chapter Nine

Tuesday morning I woke up early, and though the fog still lay curled on the surface of the lake, I could tell that in a few hours it was going to be a gorgeous day. Living in Oregon year-round, I'd gotten used to the nuances that forecast anything other than drizzle.

Remembering Erica's presence in the other room, I pulled on a seldom used terry robe and headed for the shower. Panic beat me to the door, tripping me all the way. Gammon, good-natured loaf that she was, stayed sprawled on the bed. Just as I reached the bathroom, the door opened and Erica stepped out, stark naked.

"Oh," I said.

"Sorry. I thought you were still sleeping," she said, a wry smile on her lips. She made no attempt to cover herself up but moved to the left at the same time I did, then we both dodged to the right in an awkward attempt to let the other pass. Finally Erica laughed and held up both hands in mock surrender. "I'll stay right here. You go first."

"Thank you," I said, feeling the familiar blush ride up my cheeks. Try as I might, it was impossible to ignore the way Erica's breasts, full and round, seemed to beckon me. My gaze slid down her lean, taut body, settling for a second on the glossy black triangle below her tan line. The moment lasted an eternity and I felt a stirring deep within me, a longing that had never quite gone away. I closed my eyes and stepped around her, shutting the bathroom door behind me. I turned the tap to several degrees cooler than I generally like and stepped into the shower, willing the image of Erica's damp body from my mind, blocking out the lingering hunger I felt in the center of my being.

To my delight, Erica had coffee and breakfast waiting for me, and neither of us mentioned our encounter in the hallway. Instead, we made our plans for the day, called Bart and were soon roaring across the lake in my Seaswirl. We were wearing our hiking gear and carrying backpacks loaded with binoculars and other assorted necessities, including my Colt forty-five.

Bart answered the door dressed and ready to go. He'd agreed to take the day off from working on big rigs and motor homes, saying that business was slow anyway. His red hair was tied back in a ponytail and the Yankees cap he wore with the bill facing backwards made him look like a high-school kid. It was amazing how just by shaving his head and piercing a few facial features, Buck had lost all the innocent youth that Bart projected. It was more than the way they looked, though. The differences ran deep and were reflected in their eyes. Bart had the keen, trusting eyes of a playful puppy, whereas Buck's seemed more like a Rottweiler's. But remembering the photo in Buck's drawer, I knew it hadn't always been that way.

"He may not be up there, you know," Bart said, climbing into the back of my Jeep Cherokee. "I haven't seen him since yesterday morning, when he was passed out on the sofa, but that doesn't mean he's camped out up there. He could be at a girl's house." Bart's voice held no conviction.

"When the police find out it was Buck who trashed Tommy's place, you think they're going to believe he didn't have something to do with attacking him? It's better for Buck if we do find him first." We'd already been over this, but Bart still had misgivings about leading us to his brother. I could tell he was torn. Part of him wanted to know the truth. The other part wanted to protect his brother at all costs. From what he'd told me of his past, I knew this was a familiar pattern. Bart had probably spent his childhood covering for Buck's exploits, often as not taking the fall himself. I wasn't positive, but I had the feeling Bart was getting tired of his role in the relationship.

Once outside of town, we headed northeast on an old logging road that was badly rutted and barely passable due to the encroachment of wild blackberry bushes along both sides. The road twisted and turned through the new-growth forest as we climbed steadily, leaving Cedar Hills and Rainbow Lake far below us.

"You can see the ocean from up here pretty soon," Bart volunteered from the back seat. "Just look back over your shoulder when you get to a clearing. It's pretty awesome."

"Uh, this road doesn't get any narrower, does it?" Erica asked, leaning out the passenger window. "We're pretty close to the edge."

"If Hancock's Explorer made it up here, we can. Bart, how well do you and Buck know Newt Hancock?"

"The sheriff's deputy? Just seen him around a few times, is all."

"Well, the car Tommy saw up here was his."

"Really? How do you know?"

"We found the pictures Tommy took. He was telling the truth. There was another car up there with Buck's truck and it belonged to Hancock."

"What about the note? Did you find that too?"

Erica and I had discussed whether or not to tell Bart the truth. Erica thought we should keep the note a secret for now, but for some reason, I trusted Bart. I glanced at Erica and she shrugged. I told him what we'd found.

"You don't think it's real, then?" He sounded both disappointed and relieved. If the note was phony, maybe Buck had been playing a prank after all. But I was beginning to have my doubts about whether Buck would do that.

"Okay, turn right up here," he said. "This is where the road gets kinda tricky."

"Oh, good," Erica said. By the way her nose was

glued to the window, her gaze locked on the ever-increasing distance between us and the forest floor below, I could tell she wasn't enjoying the drive much. As promised, the road became increasingly tricky, and soon we were crawling along at a snail's pace, the tires grinding in the potholes, churning to keep purchase as we climbed. I was beginning to think we'd gone as far as we could when suddenly we crested a hill and came to an abrupt halt. Buck's green pickup was parked fifty feet ahead.

"He's up here," Bart said unnecessarily. "If you want, we can just wait here until he comes back to the truck. He will eventually." It didn't sound like waiting around appealed to Bart any more than it did me.

"Is this the end of the road?"

"Nah, it goes on a long way, but it's not too good for cars, even with four-wheel drive. It's better to walk in from here. But if he's off the road a ways, we could walk right past him and not even know it. The best way is to hike up to one of the ledges and look for him through the binoculars." Bart had described the ledges, granite platforms rising above the ridge that defined the north side of the forest. From a ledge, we could see everything, he promised, including the ocean to the west. "The only problem is, it's kinda tricky gettin' there."

"Oh, good," Erica said. "Another tricky part. It can't be any worse than getting up here. Let's go for it."

That's what I liked about Erica. Always game for adventure, even when scared witless. I remembered, somewhat belatedly, that Erica was afraid of heights.

"You sure you wouldn't rather wait here?" I asked.

She rolled her eyes at me and hitched up her backpack. "Just lead the way."

And so we took off up a barely discernible trail used more by wild animals than humans. With Bart leading and Erica bringing up the rear, we climbed the steep and winding trail.

By the time we reached the first ledge, we were climbing on all fours, barely able to pull ourselves up. All three of us were panting, and sweat rolled off our faces.

"This should do it," Bart said, scrambling onto the granite ledge that jutted out over the forest floor hundreds of feet below. The ledge was four or five feet wide and ten times as long. It was the first of many such outcroppings, and from a distance they resembled stepping stones for giants. The three of us collapsed on the cool hard rock and slipped off our backpacks. Erica dug in hers for water and passed out the plastic bottles. Bart squirted his over his head, then drank thirstily. Never one to eschew a good idea when I see one, I followed suit.

"This isn't bad, as long as you don't look down," Erica said, inching closer to the edge. "Jeez! I had no idea we were this far up!"

"Cool, huh? Look over there!" Bart pointed west and the glistening blue of the Pacific Ocean winked back at us.

"I don't quite see what good it's going to do us, finding Buck from up here," she said. "When we go back down, we'll never find the spot."

"Actually, that's not true," Bart said. "When I found the bandana the other day, I figured out a system. Hold your hand up like this." He held up his hand, fingers splayed. "Now pick a tree, any tree and move your fingers until you've covered five trees. See? Now move to the next five. It's an easy way to judge distance. Once you look through the binoculars, you'll see what I mean. The logging road is real easy to see from up here. It winds right through the forest. Buck won't be far off the road. All we've got to do is find him, then use our fingers to mark off the number of trees from the road. And there are lots of landmarks once you start looking for them. Here, take a look."

Bart passed Erica a pair of binoculars and I got out my own. Suddenly, I saw what he meant. The old road was clearly etched in the forest floor, an ugly brown scar running zigzags through the trees.

"Now, let's all focus on a landmark. See the spot where they didn't log, where the trees are twice as tall? Let's use that to start with." He waited until we found the spot, then walked us through a few practice drills, showing us again how to use our hands to mark distances. Soon, Erica and I were as quick as Bart at locating landmarks, measuring off space in recognizable increments and communicating intelligently with each other regarding location and distance between various points. Once we were sure we had the hang of it, we divided up the forest and began systematically scanning it for signs of Buck.

Bart hadn't mentioned the bandana again and I suspected he was hesitant to give away its location. Still, I found myself searching as much for a glimpse of red as I was for Buck, curious to know what it was he'd really seen. It couldn't have actually been the bandana. Maybe what he'd seen was a red-tailed hawk, or a fragment of a red balloon caught on a branch. But he seemed so positive, I hated to mention these possibilities.

Five minutes into our search, Bart swore under his breath.

"What's wrong?"

"It's gone. Buck musta found it."

"The bandana? Maybe you just can't see it from here."

"No, I had it memorized. I'm positive. It's gone." He sighed, wiped his brow and resumed his search for Buck.

"Could it have been something else?" I asked gently. "A red-tailed hawk, maybe?"

"Cass, I know you think I'm crazy, but I know what I saw. It was a red bandana."

Though the sun beat down on us, the breeze from the ocean cooled our sweat and the granite ledge was almost cold. It was hard work, holding the binoculars for so long, and soon my eyes were fatigued as well. I was thinking of resting them when suddenly Erica yelped, startling me so badly I almost dropped the binoculars.

"Got him!"

"Where?" Bart and I both asked. I refocused my binoculars and followed Erica's excited instructions, using our counting system.

"He's still climbing. About twenty feet up. Look! I think he's stopping!"

Just as I zeroed in on the distant figure scaling the towering fir tree, Bart swore.

"Son of a bitch," he intoned.

"What?"

"It's not him."

"I thought he looked different," Erica said. "Unless Buck grew a head of hair overnight."

In the distance, it was difficult to see clear details

but I could make out dark clothing and, as Erica pointed out, dark hair. Buck's gleaming pate would've stood out like a beacon.

"He's coming back down," Erica said.

"Can you see who it is?" I asked.

"Not unless he turns around," Erica said.

"Can't tell from here," Bart added. "Whoa. Now that's weird. Look at that!"

"He's got the bandana!" Erica said.

"Yeah, but he's not bringing it down *from* the tree," I said. "He's putting it *in* the tree."

The three of us watched as the figure secured the red bandana to a branch, then scampered down the trunk, disappearing momentarily from our view.

"I don't get it," Bart said. "Why would someone —"

His thought went unfinished because I cut him off. "There's his car!" I'd scanned back to the base of the ridge where we'd parked, then followed the road past Buck's truck to a bend in the road. I could just barely glimpse the gleam of a metallic bumper and a flash of white beneath the firs.

"He got here before Buck? Buck must know he's up here then," Bart said.

"Not necessarily," I pointed out. "He could've come after Buck, driven past his truck as far as he could go, then walked the rest of the way in."

"But who is he?" Erica asked. "And what in the world is he doing?"

"Let's go find out!" I said. "If we hurry, we might get back down before he reaches his car."

Words of optimism if ever there were any. Climbing down proved much more difficult than the climb up. The process was made even more treacherous by Erica's abject terror. Going up, she'd managed to avoid looking down, but there was no ignoring the vast space between us and the forest floor now that we were facing it.

"You guys go on ahead. I'll get there eventually," she said bravely.

I wondered how anyone could look that good with sweat running down her forehead and terror etched on her face.

"Why don't you go down, Bart. I'll stay back with Erica."

"Okay." He didn't sound too keen on the idea. "What should I do, though, when I see him?"

"Stall him. Make chitchat. Pretend you're an innocent hiker. Whatever you do, don't confront him. But get a good look at his plates."

"What if it's someone I know?"

"Even better. Just act surprised to see him, but not too interested. Like two hikers running into each other on the trail. No big deal."

We watched Bart scurry down the path, then I turned back to Erica.

"It's probably easier if you don't look down."

"Yeah, right. Down is where we're going. How do I not look down?"

"Tell you what. I'm going to stay one step ahead of you. You just step where I do, and don't look at anything but my backside."

Despite her anxiety, Erica laughed. "You know how long I've waited for that invitation?"

"Cute, Erica. You know what I meant. Come on."

Step by step, we inched down the trail, Erica grabbing my shoulders to steady herself from time to time. We were almost to level ground when she suddenly stopped.

"Hey," she said. I turned to face her.

"Hey what?"

"Thank you." She leaned forward and brushed her lips across mine, lightly, softly, not quite innocently.

"You're welcome," I said, feeling butterflies take flight. I started to step back but Erica pulled me toward her and repeated the gesture. This time my lips parted and suddenly Erica was not just kissing me lightly. I could taste the tang of salt, feel the heat and desire that pulsed through me as she pulled me in. My eyes closed and I swayed, weak with desire, feeling the tortuously sweet softness of her lips, longing to touch her, to pull her down onto the forest floor and make love to her.

I backed away, embarrassed by the shallowness of my breathing, the flush of my skin.

"Oh, Cass," she said. "If you had any idea . . ."

"Shh," I said, putting a finger to her lips. Because I did have a pretty good idea and it scared the hell out of me. I had vowed never to fall for anyone like Erica again. Especially not Erica herself. I had sworn it! And now, just one kiss and I was ready to melt like some damned teenager. "Come on. Bart can't hold the guy forever." I turned away and marched down the path, aware that Erica was having trouble keeping up with the faster pace, but not daring to slow again, afraid I'd lose all resolve and do something stupid like ask her to move in.

When we got to the car, Bart was sitting on the hood, a lopsided grin on his face. The binoculars dangled from his wrist and it occurred to me that he'd probably been watching us on the trail.

"Well?" I asked, embarrassed.

"Dude was gone before I got down. He must've been running. I would've followed after him, but you have the keys."

"So now what?" Erica asked.

"You still wanna wait for Buckie?"

"I'm afraid your brother's not the one who's been pulling pranks," I said. "Someone out there is playing some weird game and Buck is just caught up in it. Until we know who he is, I don't think we're going to know what happened to Tommy."

"So we find the dude in the white car?"

"The dirty white car," I corrected. "With a Triple A sticker on the bumper."

"You saw that?" Erica asked, impressed.

"Well, I saw the edge of a blue circle. Triple A is all I can think of. Come on. He can't be that far ahead of us."

We piled into the Jeep and I took the road as fast as I dared, making Erica's day complete, I was sure. But when I looked over, she didn't seem to be as petrified as she had been on the way up. Maybe the hike had tamed some of her acrophobia. Or maybe, I thought wryly, it was the kiss.

"Don't think we're gonna catch him," Bart offered from the back. As it turned out, he was right.

Once back in civilization, I cruised the streets of

Cedar Hills, hoping to find a dirty white car with a round blue circle on the bumper parked somewhere along the way, but it wasn't our day. Finally admitting defeat, I offered to buy them both a drink at Lizzie's and headed for Main Street.

Chapter Ten

Lizzie's is really named Logger's Tavern, but no one calls it that. Lizzie Thompson, a tall, raw-boned woman with biceps the size of small hams, was a friend of mine, and she waved us in, making one of her regulars move over so there'd be room for the three of us at the bar.

"The usual?" she asked Bart.

He nodded, and Lizzie looked at me. "I've got one bottle of Cabernet in back and an open Chardonnay that's been in the fridge about two weeks."

"I'd kill for a beer, Lizzie. Whatever's on tap."

"How about you?" she asked, winking at Erica. Lizzie clearly remembered the nature of my relationship with Erica the last time we'd been in the tavern together. In fact, Lizzie seemed to keep tabs on my lovelife, and the grin she shot me told me she was glad to see Erica back in town.

"Beer's fine for me too," Erica said. "How are you, Lizzie?"

"Five hundred dollars poorer than I was this morning." She poured our beers and leaned her elbows on the bar, waiting for one of us to bite.

"Why's that?" I obliged.

" 'Cause that's what the damned deductible on my insurance policy is. Hell, I probably could've got the place fixed cheaper than that myself." She pointed her chin at the ceiling, indicating a blackened circle on the rafters.

"You mean that fire last month? They're just getting around to fixing it now?" I asked. The beer was ice-cold and slid down my throat nicely.

"What happened?" Erica asked.

"She nearly got the place burned down, is what," Bart volunteered.

Lizzie nodded. "Bird's nest in the chimney caught fire about a month ago. Least that's what the chimney sweep told me was the problem. Said I was lucky it hadn't happened sooner, as dirty as the thing was. He said it looked like it hadn't been cleaned since it was built, about fifty years ago. And guess what I found out today?" Lizzie waited expectantly.

"What?" Erica finally prompted.

"The last owner left a security camera up in the

rafters. The insurance guy found it. Said it looked like a good camera, too. Not that I would know the difference. I wonder why the turkey never told me."

"Maybe he was keeping an eye on his bartenders, making sure they weren't cheating him," Bart said.

"Yeah. But the insurance adjustor told me the thing was pointed right at the bar. Right where you're sitting, as a matter of fact. I'd call old Ed up and ask him about it, but he's dead."

"You sure the old owner's the one who put it there?" I asked.

"Well, *I* sure didn't. I can barely aim a Kodak Instamatic. Wait'll you see this thing. Just a sec." She disappeared behind the bar and returned, holding a silver video camera in both hands. "Pretty fancy for old Ed," she said.

"Lizzie, that's an understatement. This thing is state-of-the-art by *today's* standards," I said, examining the equipment. "You've owned this place for what? Ten years? I don't think old Ed's the one who hid this camera in the rafters."

"But who else?" she asked, suddenly looking worried. "I mean, no one can even get in here without my knowing, let alone up in the rafters. Kelly, the one who tends bar on Friday's, is the only other one with a key."

"Maybe Kelly's got a jealous boyfriend who likes to keep his eye on her while she works," I said.

"That's sick," Bart noted.

"Yeah, but it's feasible. I mean, she doesn't lock the key in a safe at night, right? So someone could get ahold of it."

"She doesn't even have a boyfriend," Lizzie insisted, not wanting to believe that her sanctuary had been violated.

"How about workers? Delivery men? Any chance someone could've got up there when you were in back, maybe in the morning before opening?"

Lizzie was shaking her head, looking more disconsolate by the minute. "I get deliveries on Wednesdays, right in back. They don't even come through here. And look at this place. Does it look like I've had a lot of workers in here?"

"How about the chimney sweep? After the fire?"

Lizzie's eyes narrowed. She started to speak, then pursed her lips, thinking. She looked at me, then glanced around the bar before speaking. When she did, her voice was low. "It's possible. It doesn't make sense, but it's possible."

A lot of stuff had been happening lately that didn't make sense. No reason Lizzie should be exempt, I thought. For some reason, the little hairs on my arms were standing up, a sensation that often preceded a sudden revelation. It was like knowing I knew something but not knowing what it was I knew. "Who swept the chimney?" I asked, trying to make myself concentrate on one thing at a time.

"Guy Waddell. You know him? Works odd jobs and such. Lives out at Professor Cathwaite's on the lake. He fixed my electric stove at home a while back. Comes in here once a month to load the Cathwaites' liquor order."

I raised an eyebrow and she explained.

"They throw lots of parties, I guess. I know the professor holds a weekly gaming club out there, too. Anyway, it's easier for them to load right onto their boat from the dock here than to buy it at the liquor store. They're not the only ones who buy from me. The price is the same and for those without road access, I'm more convenient. Anyway, that's how I first met Guy. He comes in for a beer now and then, too."

Something was bothering me, but I was so focused on Guy Waddell that it took me a minute to realize what it was. Suddenly, it came together.

"Ginny Cathwaite's the professor's wife?" I asked. Ginny Cathwaite had checked out the book about The Rainbow Ridge treasure right after Tommy had.

"That's her. Bouncy little thing. Perky, I guess you'd call her. But sharp-tongued as all get out. She bosses that Guy around like he's her personal slave."

"And when did Guy do the chimney?"

"I had him do it on a Sunday right after the fire. He said the job was too messy to do during business hours. I let him in around ten and came back an hour later. He was still up there, sooty from head to foot."

"What are you thinking, Cass?" Erica asked. I held up my hand, trying to concentrate.

"And how long ago was this?"

"A little over a month ago."

Right before Tommy, the professor's wife and some old bearded man in expensive clothes checked out the books. Just after Tommy and the Bailey boys met an old bearded man in Lizzie's tavern who told a tall tale about the lost treasure. I felt like someone staring at a jumbled jigsaw puzzle, knowing the pieces somehow fit together, but unable to imagine the finished picture. I turned to Bart.

"That night you guys met the old man in here, where were you sitting?"

"Right here, where we always do. The old guy was sitting where you are. And you know what? For what it's worth, I think Guy Waddell was in here that night, too. But he was over there playing pool, mostly. Why?"

I described the old man to Lizzie and asked if she remembered him.

"That was Kelly's night. But he doesn't sound the least bit familiar to me. Musta been new in town. What's the old man got to do with Guy Waddell and why would Guy put a camera in my ceiling rafters?"

"I'm not sure, Lizzie. Mind if I borrow that camera?"

"Hell, you can have it, Cass. The adjustor told me it's no good without the other part. Apparently this thing is remote-activated from somewhere else. By itself, it isn't even any good. Not that I understand how it works."

But I did. Somewhere, someone was watching the happenings at Lizzie's bar on their own television. And if it wasn't Guy Waddell, then it was a good bet he knew who it was. The professor? His wife? The old man? I may not have known the answers, but at least now I knew some of the right questions to ask. The main one, of course, was why? Why on earth did anyone give a rat's ass what went on in Lizzie's bar? I had a feeling I wasn't going to like the answer when I found it.

I drained my beer and asked Lizzie one more question, my fingers crossed for luck. "How do the Cathwaites pay when they order from you? Cash, credit card? How does that work?"

"Well, Mrs. Cathwaite usually signs for the order while Guy loads the boat. I bill them by mail and she sends in a check once a month. Always on time, I might add."

"You wouldn't happen to have one of those checks handy, would you?"

"No, but I've got this month's order forms. Would that help?"

I told her it might and she went to get it. Several minutes later she returned and handed me a slip of paper.

"Ho, ho, ho!" I said.

"What?" all three asked simultaneously.

"What do you want to bet that Mrs. Cathwaite is domineering and insensitive?"

"Why's that?" Bart asked.

"Because the crossbar on her *T* is heavier than on the stem."

"Huh?" Lizzie said.

"The note," Erica said. "The professor's wife is the one who forged Tommy's note!" She was as excited as I was.

"You've lost me," Lizzie complained.

"I'll explain later," I said, taking the camera with me. "Buy Bart all the beer he wants, on me."

"Oh, no, you don't. I'm coming too." Bart stood up, looking defiant.

"Oh, what the hell. Come on. Lizzie, the second we've got this figured out, you'll be the first to know."

"Yeah, right." She was clearly miffed, but I didn't have time to explain. I headed for the Jeep, Erica and Bart on my heels.

Chapter Eleven

The minute we got to my place, Bart and I jumped in the lake to wash away the grit of the hike. Erica opted for a shower. Now we were sprawled on the front deck, sipping icy Coronas. I didn't really mind Bart's presence. It saved me from acting on feelings I didn't care to acknowledge — feelings that refused to stay down where I'd buried them. Bart provided a buffer, but besides that, I liked him. I could see why Tommy and he had bonded. They were both guileless, both good-natured, both big-hearted. At the moment, Bart was giggling like a kid.

"You think I ought to tell him?"

"Oh, I don't know, Bart." Erica said. "If you don't tell him, he's liable to spend days and days climbing those trees chasing phony notes."

Bart giggled again.

"Yeah, it sure would be a shame," I chimed in. "Poor old Buck sweating up those trees when the whole time there never was any treasure."

Bart tried to get the giggles under control, but it was a struggle. "It wouldn't be very nice," he said.

"No," Erica agreed. "Poor Buckie."

"But it would kind of serve him right," I said.

Bart gave up the struggle and let himself go. His laughter was infectious. "Ooh-whee! Would it serve him right!" He snorted. He was clearly enjoying the thought of finally one-upping his brother. "But I couldn't wait very long. Just a few days maybe."

"Right," Erica said.

"Or a week at the most."

"Definitely no longer than a month," I said.

"Boy, this is gonna be fun!" Bart said.

Somehow, I didn't think Bart would be able to hold out very long. I gave him a day, maybe two, before his conscience got the better of him.

"Hey, Bart. Something I've been wondering. Are you and Buck the only kids, or do you have brothers and sisters?"

I hadn't told Bart about my uninvited visit to their home, so he didn't know I'd seen the picture.

"Just us," he said. He was still reclined in the chaise lounge, but his body stiffened and all the fun drained from his tone. I waited, wondering what had happened to the girl in the picture. The silence hung between us awkwardly. Finally, he sat up. "We had a sister, but she died."

I pictured the little Shirley Temple in Buck's arms, remembered the way he'd looked at her. "What happened?"

"Long story," he said. He looked up, and to my surprise, there were tears in his eyes. He took a long pull on his bottle and stared out at the lake. "My old man caught my mom in bed with the next-door neighbor. He beat the crap outta the guy, then beat the crap outta my mom, grabbed Leslie and took off."

He paused, like that explained everything.

"Your father kidnaped your sister?"

"Tried to. Buck and me were just coming home from school when we saw them go by. Leslie was pressed against the window screaming for help and we saw my dad backhand her. Buck was always braver than me, but he was still afraid of my father. But when we saw him hit Leslie that day, Buck went ballistic. He took off after them, running down the street screaming at him to stop and let Leslie out. He almost caught up to them, too, because there was a stoplight at the end of the block. But when my old man saw Buck about to catch up, he gunned it right through the intersection. And that's how Leslie died."

He took a deep breath and I realized he'd barely breathed as the words tumbled out in a rush. His cheeks were blotched with emotion and his eyes were wet.

"And your father?"

"They both died in the crash. I wish my father had lived, though, as much as I hated him. Then Buck could've blamed my father instead of . . ." His voice trailed off.

"Instead of what, Bart?"

"Instead of blaming himself for the crash. It's hard to hate someone who's dead. You know what I mean?"

I thought I did. Buck had turned the anger and hatred he felt for his father toward himself. In one day, Bart Bailey had lost his little sister, his father and, for all intents and purposes, his twin brother. Buck had become a walking time bomb and Bart had spent the years ever since trying to stop his brother from self-destructing.

"That's a pretty heavy load you're bearing," Erica said.

Bart looked up, his brow furrowed. "What do you mean?"

"You know what I mean, Bart. You let Buck walk all over you because you're afraid if you stand up to him, he might just storm off, and you're all he's got. So you put up with it."

Bart was staring at her wide-eyed, shaking his head. "No. You don't understand. I mean, at least Buck tried to stop him. At least he did something! All I did was yell at Buck to slow down. I was afraid my father would turn around and come after us! I was the coward and Buck knows it. But he thinks I blame him for the accident. Which I don't! I never did. Oh, God. It's so fucking complicated, it makes me sick." By now, Bart had wrapped his arms around his knees and was rocking back and forth.

"You ever talk to someone about this?" I asked gently.

"You mean, like a shrink? Yeah, back in junior high. I went. Buck wouldn't go. Mom tried to make him, but by then no one could make Buck do anything. Especially not her. As much as he blamed himself for causing the crash, he blamed her for having the affair. None of us survived that day, if you want to know the truth. I understand this stuff better than you think. I just can't seem to do anything to change it."

"You think about going again? Now that you're an adult?"

He looked up, narrowed his eyes at me, then nodded. "Yeah, actually. I do think about it. You know, except for Tommy, you guys are the only ones I've ever said this stuff to, except the shrink in junior high. For novices, you're not bad. I actually feel a little better." He grinned, but I knew the pain he felt was simmering just below the surface.

"I know someone," I said, thinking of Maggie. "I'll give you her number. She's good." I ignored Erica's raised brow at that comment and went inside, leaving the two of them on the deck.

Through the window, I could see them talking and knew they'd changed the subject by the occasional laughter and lighter tones coming through the glass. I busied myself with gathering notecards, butcher paper, Scotch tape and colored pens. I taped the butcher paper to the living room window and started making notes on cards. By the time Bart and Erica came in to see what I was doing, I had a dozen notecards taped onto the butcher paper under two headings: *Questions* and *Answers.*

"Whatcha doin'?" Bart asked, his good-natured demeanor restored.

"Trying to make sense out of this mess. What do you think?"

Under *QUESTIONS* I had taped several entries. *Who attacked Tommy and why? Why did Ginny Cathwaite forge the Lost Treasure note? What was Newt Hancock doing up on Rainbow Ridge? Who was leaving phony clues on trees and why? Who was the old man in the library? Who was the old man in the tavern? Were they the same person? Was it really Guy Waddell who put a video camera in Lizzie's tavern? If so, who was watching the video? Who was following Erica and why? What do Hancock, Guy, the old man and Ginny Cathwaite have in common?*

"That one's the key," Erica said, pointing to the last question.

"You could be right."

"Now all you need's the answers," Bart quipped.

"That's where you come in, Bart. We're going to play a game. Get comfy, guys."

The three of us settled around the living room and proceeded to brainstorm.

"Whatever comes off the top of your head," I said. "No fair taking too much time. Just blurt out your first thought. Okay. Why did someone attack Tommy? I'll take anything."

"To get the fake clue," Bart said.

"To get the picture of Hancock's car."

I glanced at Erica, writing their answers on cards in a hurried scrawl. "What was Hancock doing up there?"

"Checking up on Buck. Maybe he followed him there and thought he was up to no good."

Erica shook her head. "No. I bet he's in on the scam, somehow. Maybe he's the one planting the clues."

"He drives a black Explorer. The guy in the tree today had a white car," I said.

"So, maybe they take turns," Bart said.

I wrote furiously, going through notecards. "This is good, guys. Okay. What's Mrs. Cathwaite's role in this?"

"She bosses Guy Waddell around. He works for the Cathwaites. So he put the video cam up there at her instruction."

"Good, Erica. Why?"

They both looked at me blankly.

"No fair thinking. Just blurt something out."

"She's a pervert. She likes to lie in bed and watch strange men get drunk at the bar," Erica said, looking embarrassed.

Bart giggled. "She's making movies. Only, the stars of the movies don't know they're being taped. Like Candid Camera."

I quit writing and stared at Bart.

"I know, I know. But you said to just blurt something out."

"No. Go on with that. That's really good. What kind of movies?"

"Real ones," Erica said. "Slices of small-town life."

"Boring ones," Bart said, laughing.

"So maybe they're too boring and she makes things happen?" I said.

"Like what?" Erica asked.

"Like the old guy in the bar. Maybe he was a plant."

"I don't get it," Bart said.

"Okay. Pretend this old guy's an actor. He goes to the library, does his research, then goes to the bar and delivers his lines. The camera gets the whole scene on tape. Only you guys don't know you're part of the play."

"Boring!" Bart said again.

"Not really, Bart," Erica said. "Think about it. What that guy told you started a whole string of events. Your brother tried to cheat you, Tommy tried to confront Buck, Hancock followed Buck to the ridge, someone attacked Tommy. Not boring at all."

"But if it's only a game, why did someone try to kill Tommy? I don't know. It seems pretty far-fetched to me. You think Hancock is one of the actors too?" Bart asked.

"Let's change direction for a minute. What do Hancock, Guy and the old man have in common?"

They both thought, came up with nothing.

"Well, let's start by listing what we know. First the old man."

"He was dying," Bart said.

"He *said* he was dying," Erica corrected. "If we assume he was acting then the whole story could've been part of the act. But if the guy the librarian described was also the man in the bar then we know something about how he really is, assuming he wasn't play-acting in the library."

"Right," I said. "Sharp dresser. Monied. She thought maybe he was a retired doctor. The type to read Shakespeare."

"Sophisticated," Erica said.

"Rich," Bart added.

"Describe Hancock," I said, making notes.

"Vain. Womanizer. A snake," Erica said.

"Sharp dresser?" I prompted.

"Definitely. And well-off."

"So they do have something in common!" Bart said.

"Yeah, maybe they met at Nordstrom's," Erica teased.

"Okay, forget it. Let's go on. What do we know about Guy?"

"Not a sharp dresser," Bart said. "Every time I've seen him, he's wearing jeans and a T-shirt. Skinny guy but strong."

"Works odd jobs, but lives at the Cathwaites'. Maybe he and Mrs. Cathwaite have a thing going," Erica said.

"What about Mr. Cathwaite? Where is he in all this?"

"He's a professor," I said, suddenly thinking of something. "You know what? I think he was at the park when Tommy was attacked. Remember the guy who gave his shirt to Booker? Booker called him Professor. Could be the same guy."

"I remember him," Erica said. "Yellow tennis shirt."

"He's rich, right?" Bart asked. "So he and Hancock and the old man all have money."

"But not Guy," Erica said.

"But Guy works for the professor, right?"

"Right." We all sat wondering where to go next.

"I think we're stuck," Bart finally said.

"We need to find out who drives that white car," I said to Bart. "You think you can take another day off work?"

"You want me to try and track it down?"

“The town’s not that big. It’s worth a shot.”

“He could live in Kings Harbor, though.”

I looked at him, not needing the pessimism.

“Okay. Okay. I’ll do it.”

“Good. Erica, you think you can cozy up to Newt Hancock?”

“Are you kidding? The problem won’t be turning him on. It’ll be turning him off.”

Bart laughed.

“So what do you want me to find out?” Erica asked.

“Whatever you can without being obvious. If he knows the Cathwaites. If he knows Guy. What he was doing up on the ridge. Anything you can think of that will help explain his part in this. But be careful. He absolutely can not know you’re grilling him.”

“Oh, right. ‘Gee, Newt. What nice biceps you have. Get those climbing Rainbow Ridge by any chance?’ ”

“You’ll think of something.”

“What are you going to do?” Bart asked.

“Find out everything I can about the good professor. His wife forges the note, his handyman installs surveillance equipment in Lizzie’s bar, and he’s right there in the thick of things when Tommy gets attacked. Something about the way he offered his shirt that day. I don’t know. Maybe he wanted to be close to Tommy, to make sure he wasn’t talking.”

“Speaking of Tommy, we should call,” Erica said. The three of us looked at each other guiltily. For a few minutes, we’d almost forgotten the reason for our investigation. While Bart and Erica called, I taped up more notecards on the chart and stood back, wondering whether the brainstorm session had gotten us any closer to the truth, or if it had led us down the wrong path completely. When they came back into the living room, they were grim-faced.

"No change," Erica said. "Tommy's still in a coma."

Chapter Twelve

It was a relief to wake up Wednesday morning to an empty house. Erica had decided it was safe enough to return to her house and Bart volunteered to sleep on her sofa, just in case. I think in reality he was just afraid to go back to his place and face Buck. At any rate, the cats were glad to be rid of Pepper and I didn't have to worry about running into a naked Erica in the hallway.

After feeding Panic and Gammon, I went through my daily exercise routine, watered the flowers on my back patio, spent a little time in the greenhouse pulling weeds, then went in to make a light breakfast. By nine o'clock, I was ready to face the day.

Kings Harbor Community College sits on one of the prettiest pieces of real estate along the Oregon coast. The Pacific Ocean can be seen through the cedar and fir trees that line the towering sand dunes on the west side of campus. I'd once spent a month posing as a drama student there and was familiar with the buildings and layout of the campus. That morning I parked in front of the administration building and went inside to get a course list for summer classes and a look at the faculty roster.

According to the roster, Professor Cathwaite had a Ph.D. in behavioral science from N.Y.U. and a Master's in psychology from Boston University. I wondered what a big east-coast academic was doing way out west teaching at a small-town community college. The only class he was teaching that summer was an introductory social science class for freshmen, held Tuesday through Thursday from eleven to twelve. If I hurried, I could swing by the library for a look at his dissertation, then pop into the lecture hall for a glimpse of the man in action before meeting Martha for lunch.

The college library was small but well-stocked and had a comfortable, relaxed atmosphere. The librarian was a young gay man who was happy to help me find Professor Cathwaite's dissertation, as well as a book he'd written with another local professor named Kip Cage. Maybe that's why Cathwaite had come out west — to work with Cage on the book. I took the two documents to an overstuffed easy chair and settled in for what I assumed would be a dull and dreary dose of academic mumbo-jumbo.

To my surprise, the dissertation was anything but dull and dreary. Not only could Professor Cathwaite write, but his ideas were rather avant garde, as the title — *Predicting Human Behavior: A Study in Probability and Personality Traits* — suggested. I began by thumbing through the pages but was soon reading every word. Halfway through, I put the dissertation aside and picked up the professor's book. The title, *Free Will?*, was even more intriguing than the dissertation. I scanned the table of contents and saw that the book was an elaboration on the earlier thesis, but the professor had taken his ideas a step further.

He began by boldly asserting that despite most people's belief that they retained some control over their own actions, they were in fact victims of probability, slaves to their own nature. He dedicated several chapters to the debate over nature versus nurture, then set the argument aside, stating that it made no difference how a person arrived at their character. As adults, he opined, they were locked into predictable patterns, their actions practically foregone conclusions in almost any situation.

To prove his theory, he had used an unwitting class of graduate students as his control group, assessed each one's IQ and personality traits based on a series of tests including the standard Rorschach, Stanford-Binet and handwriting analysis, then accurately predicted each student's response to various stimuli over the course of a semester. The little hairs on my arms and neck were standing straight up as I read how he'd purposely set a fire in the classroom to prove how particular students would respond to the emergency, how he'd purposely placed the answers to a test out in the open so he could prove which students would cheat and which ones wouldn't — the list went on and on.

As I scanned the pages with a sense of horrid fascination, I kept picturing the surveillance equipment in Lizzie's bar, taping the way Tommy, Bart and Buck responded to an old man's tale of lost treasure in the hills. Were they nothing more than fodder for this man's next book? Or was something else going on entirely? Either way, if it was the professor who'd been secretly taping the tavern, then something had gone terribly wrong and Tommy was in the thick of it. I looked at my watch and hurried out of the library toward the lecture hall and Professor Cathwaite's eleven o'clock class.

The second I saw him, I recognized him from the festival at the park. Tall and lean, with a well-trimmed beard showing white at the edges, he had fashionably short-cut brown hair, graying at the temples, and gray, penetrating eyes. He was dressed casually in tan trousers, brown leather Docksiders and a pale orange cotton polo shirt. He stood at a lectern addressing a half-full lecture hall. Those in attendance seemed riveted, and it wasn't long before I too was caught up in the professor's enthusiasm.

I'd hoped to catch him talking about the subject of his book, but instead he was discussing the previous night's reading assignment, an article on gender development and sexual preference. Males and females alike seemed shaken by his notions — radical to them — that in a different society with a different set of mores, it was perfectly reasonable to assume that the vast majority of the people in that room would be bisexual. I could tell he enjoyed their shocked objections, and in fact seemed to incite them deliberately, drawing them into the heated debate. I was beginning to think that his lecture seemed almost antithetical to his thesis on free will, when he announced to the class that their shocked reactions were entirely predictable. The room fell silent for a moment, as if the students had been insulted into submission.

"Who is going to challenge me on this?" he taunted. A few tentative hands shot up and soon the lively debate raged on. Far from the boring lecture I'd expected, Professor Cathwaite conducted a fast-paced, emotionally charged give-and-take that had everyone in the room poised on the edge of their seats. When the campus bells chimed at noon, not one person got up to leave.

"Well, I guess, we'll have to wait and finish this discussion tomorrow," he said. It was the first time I'd ever heard college freshmen groan at having to leave class.

Both energized and intrigued, I filed out with the rest of them. There was no doubt the professor was charismatic, intelligent and passionate about his work. He also had somewhat unconventional ideas, and he didn't hesitate to rile people up. He'd clearly known how the students would react to his assertions about bisexuality and he'd purposely egged them on. Just as he'd known how his graduate students would react to the variables he'd laid out for them in his doctoral thesis, I thought. He didn't seem to have any qualms about using human subjects for his experiments back in 1975 or for his own enjoyment now. The one thing I was absolutely sure of was that Professor Cathwaite had been enjoying himself in there. The students may have been curious and even riveted, but the professor was having sheer fun.

I spent the short drive to The Salad Palace mulling over potential scenarios, wondering exactly what the professor was up to and how he'd come to choose Tommy and his friends as guinea pigs. The way I figured it, Bart hadn't been far off. But it wasn't the professor's wife making her version of weird home movies, it was the professor himself conducting sociological experiments using tavern-goers as his subjects. But what was the point? And how had it gotten so far out of hand that Tommy ended up in a coma?

The Salad Palace looked like a converted barn with potted ferns hanging from the rafters to hide the unfinished ceiling joists. The buffet selections were plentiful, imaginative and always fresh. Martha was waiting for me at the entrance, a tray held impatiently on her knee.

"I was about to start without you," she said, giving me a bear hug. Martha is a big woman who looks like a cop even out of uniform. If she were wearing pjs and bunny slippers, you'd still know she was the law. That day she was dressed sharply in a navy blazer and matching slacks. I knew by the familiar bulge that beneath the jacket was a holstered forty-five, and that she carried a smaller piece in an ankle strap just above her boot.

"You look good," she said, holding me at arm's-length and appraising me with a practiced eye. "You getting enough sleep?"

"Very funny, Mart. The answer is, yes. Plenty. Come on, I'm starving."

Martha laughed at her failed attempt to find out if I was sleeping with Erica and led the way, piling greens on her plate as she worked her way down the buffet. "Don't know why people think salads are dietary," she said. "By the time I put all this stuff on, I've got more fat grams than a Big Mac." She heaped on another spoonful of sunflower seeds and reached for the grated cheddar.

"There's no law that says you've got to take everything just because it's available."

She gave me a pained expression and glanced pointedly at my plate, which was every bit as full as hers. "I rest my case," she said, moving toward the blue cheese dressing.

I thought momentarily about opting for the less fattening light Italian, just to show her I could eschew a few grams of fat if I wanted to, then sighed and heaped on the blue cheese.

"So, how's the kid?" she asked, sliding into a booth.

"Still in a coma. No one seems to have any idea if he'll pull out of it or not."

"Any lead on who the doer was?"

"Well, that's a funny question, Mart. You got a few hours?"

She laughed. "Give me the *Readers Digest* version."

So I did. When I finished, Martha gave up hunting for fat grams on her plate and put her fork down. Her brown eyes regarded me with concern.

"Seems to me," she said finally, "that you've got at least two different things going on here. This Buck

Bailey character sounds like a walking menace. Could be Hancock was following him for good reason. I still like him as your perp. But this other stuff with the professor is just plain weird. There's definitely something hinky going on with him. What's Booker think?"

"Uh, I haven't really told him much, Mart."

Her eyes narrowed. "You're holding out on Tom? Why?"

"Because of Hancock. If Tom thinks for one second that his deputy is involved in what happened to Tommy, he'll go off half-cocked. He'll confront him, I know he will. I just want to buy a little time."

"So what's your plan?" she asked, reaching for her wallet.

I waved her away and put a twenty on the table. Martha had paid last time. "I'm still working on it," I said truthfully.

Martha frowned. "I'd feel better if Tom were working with you on this."

"Hey, the second I know what's happening, I'll tell him everything. I promise."

"Yeah, well, just be careful. And keep me informed, okay? Now, what's up with my favorite Glamor Girl? You handling her okay?"

"Sort of." I laughed. "She kissed me."

"And?"

"And. I kissed her back."

"Well. That *is* progress." Martha was grinning. "I was beginning to think you'd never see the light!"

"Oh, come on, Mart. You make it sound like it's a foregone conclusion that we'll get back together. I *do* have something to say about this, you know."

She threw back her head and laughed. "You do

realize that you're the only one in town who *doesn't* know you're still in love with her?"

It was my turn to laugh. "I don't know, Mart. I don't want to just fall into something without, you know, thinking it through."

"Oh, for God's sake! All you do is think things through. One of these days, you ought to just let yourself go and do what you feel like." She stood up, leaned over and kissed me on the forehead, then marched toward the exit. "Call me!" she ordered.

Around two, when I pulled into the marina parking lot, Sheriff Tom Booker was waiting for me. He stood with his black Stetson pushed back, a toothpick between his teeth like he had all the time in the world. I knew that look. The relaxed stance didn't fool me one bit.

"How come I get the feeling you're avoiding me?" he asked.

I climbed out of the Cherokee and leaned against the door. "Maybe because the last time I talked to you, you acted like a world-class butthead."

Despite himself, he chuckled. "That I did, girl. On the other hand, as I recall, you were guilty of withholding pertinent evidence in an ongoing investigation. You're lucky I didn't haul you in!"

We glared at each other for about two seconds. Then Booker threw his toothpick into the dumpster and followed me down to my boat.

"I don't have to ask you if you're up to something, because I can tell by that look in your eyes that you are. You gonna tell me what it is, or do I have to wait until you decide to grace me with another revelation?"

"Have to wait," I said, smiling sweetly. "I haven't got it quite figured out yet. How about you?"

He scowled at me, then gave in to his need to talk about it. "The Bailey boys have all but disappeared. Word has it Buck was real ticked off the other night, and his prints are all over Tommy's place, so it looks like he was in on the ransacking. I was kinda hoping you'd share with me the location of this supposed lost treasure, or whatever it is, so I could mosey on up there myself and have a talk with the boys."

"Bart's not up there, and he wasn't involved in trashing Tommy's."

"Okay." He waited, pulling another toothpick out of his shirt pocket and twirling it between his lips. You could always tell an ex-smoker. When they were agitated, they had to put something in their mouths. I thought about telling Booker everything we'd learned, calculating the risks either way. If I didn't tell him, I might actually be withholding valuable evidence — a crime, as he'd so delicately reminded me. Worse, I'd be lying to a friend. But then there was the issue of Newt. What I'd told Martha was true. If Booker thought his deputy might be involved in a crime, he'd probably confront him. As much as I owed it to Booker to be honest, I gritted my teeth, sent a silent apology to the gods and told a partial truth.

"Buck is up there, or at least I think he is. Bart took us up there yesterday, but we couldn't find him. His truck's there though. I think he's camping out." I gave Booker the general directions.

"Hmph," Booker intoned. "By 'us,' I assume you

mean you and Erica Trinidad. How do you know Bart's innocent?"

"Because I talked to him." I told Booker everything Bart had told me in the truckstop — how Tommy had found out that Buck was looking for the lost clue without them, how Tommy had found the long-lost note in Buck's backpack and taken it, and how Buck had gone postal when he found out it was missing. Every word was true. I just happened to leave out everything I'd learned since then. Namely, that the notes were phony and that from what I could gather, the professor, his wife, his handyman, maybe even Newt and who knew how many others, were playing some kind of weird game at the boys' expense. It was possible that Buck didn't have a damn thing to do with the attack on Tommy. Then again, it seemed he *had* looked up Erica's address and someone *had* followed her, probably him. I held onto that thought and tried to look at Booker with sincere innocence.

"Hmph," he said again. He looked for a place to throw his toothpick, then pocketed it and stroked his silver moustache.

"Guess I better head on up the ridge then and have a chat. You look kinda funny. Everything goin' okay out there on the lake?"

He meant with Erica.

"Yeah. Pretty much. I think so."

"Hmph," he said again. Sometimes Booker said more with monosyllabic grunts than others did with words, but from the way he was shifting his weight from foot to foot, I suspected he had something to say.

"What?" I finally asked.

"Oh, nothing, really. I was just thinking about

something I said the other day about being careful, on account of I hated to see you get hurt again. Not that it's any of my business, of course. But, well . . ."

"Tom, what in the world are you trying to tell me?"

"Well, sometimes it doesn't pay to be too careful. You know. I mean, good things don't always come around all that often. If you know what I mean." His cheeks had turned uncharacteristically pink and it was the first time I'd ever heard him stammer.

"I appreciate the advice," I said, feeling my own cheeks redden. Booker shrugged like it was no big deal and climbed into his cruiser before either of us could say anything else to embarrass ourselves.

I waited until he drove off, then walked the half-block to Lizzie's tavern.

Chapter Thirteen

"I'm not speaking to you," Lizzie informed me when I slid onto the barstool. "Something's going on and you're leaving me out in the cold!"

The bar was blessedly empty, save for a couple of guys at the pool table and one working the pinball machine.

"You're right," I said. "You have as much right to know what's going on as anyone. That's why I'm here." This softened her a bit and she leaned her elbows on the bar.

"I couldn't sleep last night," she admitted. "The

idea that someone's been spying on my customers makes me furious. It was all I could do not to throttle Guy Waddell last night. Took every ounce of restraint I had to be civil."

Which was why I was there. Lizzie knew just enough to be dangerous. It was better to have her on the team than to leave her hanging. On her own, she might do something to screw the whole thing up.

"You think you could break away from this place for a while?"

Lizzie looked around, then went to the wall phone and punched in a number. A minute later she was back, her purse slung over her shoulder. "Kelly will be here in five minutes. She just lives across the street."

"Good. You have the Cathwaites' address?"

She disappeared again and by the time she returned, Kelly was toweling glasses behind the bar.

I poked my head out the door and glanced up and down the street, making sure Booker was nowhere in sight, then led Lizzie back to my boat.

I putt-putted through the channel, giving Lizzie a rundown of what I thought was going on. Her brown eyes widened as I recounted the professor's earlier experiments with his grad students, and she immediately made the connection with what had happened in her bar.

"That's immoral!" she said indignantly. "At least if it was someone checking up on a cheating spouse or something, that I could maybe understand. But invading the privacy of my customers . . ."

"I agree. The question is, what are they using the tapes for?"

"Another book maybe?"

“Maybe,” I said, not convinced. “You ever been to the Cathwaites’ place?”

“Me? No. Never been invited. Well, except to bartend once at a party. I let Kelly do it. She’s more impressed with that stuff than I am. In fact, she’s got another job coming up this Sunday out there.”

“The Cathwaites are throwing a party this weekend?”

“Yep. My sister-in-law is helping with the catering. The last time she said they had enough food for an army.”

“Hmm. Didn’t you also say the professor hosts a weekly card game?”

“Mrs. Cathwaite referred to it as a gaming club, I believe. Every Friday night.”

“What do they play?”

“Who knows? Bridge? Poker? Fantasy football’s big with my customers. I’m not really sure. I just fill the orders. The way they go through the booze, I think they must have quite a crowd, though.”

It didn’t surprise me that I hadn’t run into the Cathwaites before. While Cedar Hills itself was practically small enough to know everyone in town, the lake was a sprawling tangle of arms that spread out along nearly fifty miles of shoreline. The lakeshore was dotted with houses of all shapes and sizes, from old log cabins to palatial estates. Many of the homes were used as weekend get-aways and summer retreats, but at last count, at least a hundred homes were lived in year-round. Residents with road access leading out to the highway could avoid the town of Cedar Hills altogether, doing their shopping and business in Kings Harbor instead.

Scattered between the larger houses were camping lots, dry cabins, and dilapidated houseboats tethered to shore. Here and there, seaplanes were nestled in the trees, moored in front of their owners' estates. Every type of boat imaginable could be found on the lake, and it was one of the few places I'd ever heard of where rich and poor lived side-by-side in relative compatibility.

When I reached the buoys indicating the end of the no-wake zone, I pushed down on the throttle, sending a white spray of water behind us, and headed for Sturgeon Bay. Situated on the southernmost arm of Rainbow Lake, the cove was a secluded, heavily treed spit of land arching between the lake and the hills behind it. I had motored along the shore of the cove many times, enjoying the wildlife and solitude. Few water-skiers ventured out this far, and despite the promising name, the cove was not known for its fishing. The few houses along the cove's shore were scattered, providing both privacy and spectacular views of the lake.

There was no numbering system for addresses on Rainbow Lake. The mailman who delivered mail three times a week by boat relied on the names posted on the mailboxes nailed to the docks. I slowed down and cruised along, until I found the mailbox that read *Cathwaite*. In retrospect, it should have been obvious. Among the half-dozen weekend cabins and summer homes was one enormous Lyndal Cedar A-frame, with spectacular triangles of glass facing the water. Wide cedar decks circled the house on both levels and a stone chimney jutted out above the green metal roof. The grounds were well-kept and the boathouse in front was large enough to accommodate a small fleet.

Tied to one end of the dock was an orange and white pontoon replete with shade canopy and wet bar. Apparently the Cathwaites had their own private party boat. I circled around, coasted out to the middle of the cove and cut the engine.

"Wow!" Lizzie said.

"Kinda big for two people," I said. "Do they have kids?"

"Don't know. But they must have lots of friends. And Guy lives out here with them, from what I understand. Great party house, huh?"

"Looks pretty secure," I said, using my binoculars to scan the grounds. Fences were almost unheard of on Rainbow Lake, but the Cathwaites, or perhaps the previous owners, had gone to considerable expense to construct a handsome stucco boundary around the perimeter of the property. "Betcha there are dogs on the other side of that fence."

"Why's that?"

"It's not tall enough to keep anyone out who really wanted to get in, otherwise. I know *he's* a professor. Any idea what she does? This place cost some serious money."

"As far as I know, she doesn't even work."

Just then, we heard the sound of another boat turning into the cove.

"Grab a fishing pole," I said, pointing Lizzie to the rear of the boat. I stuffed my binoculars under the seat and took one of the poles, casting a bare hook into the water before slowly reeling it in. The boat was a classic hand-crafted wooden v-hull in near-perfect condition, and I realized I'd seen it on the lake before. I'd never given the driver a second look, always gazing instead at the sleek, gleaming craft as I raced by. Now I could see the driver clearly. Professor Cathwaite was home from his daily lecture.

"Just keep fishing and keep your back turned," I whispered. I knew how well voices carried on the water. Without being too obvious, I kept an eye on the professor as he docked. He had donned a blue captain's hat that might've looked silly on some, but seemed to suit him. He stood at the old-fashioned steering wheel in the bow and steered the boat with one hand, taking in his surroundings. He glanced in our direction, then guided his boat toward the boathouse. The metal door slid open automatically and closed behind the sleek boat, but not before I spotted a pair of Jet Skis and a red speedboat inside. A few minutes later, I saw him walking up the ramp toward the gated entry and immediately heard the sound of joyous barking. Big dogs, probably two of them, I thought. The professor did something that made the doors whoosh open automatically. Then he turned and took a long hard look at my boat before disappearing behind the closing doors.

"He saw us," Lizzie said.

"What's to see? Two people fishing in the cove." But my heart was pounding. For a moment, I could've sworn that Professor Cathwaite had looked right through me.

"Maybe he recognized you from the lecture," Erica said.

"Or the county park," Bart offered.

We were back on my front deck sipping a half-frozen concoction that Lizzie had whipped up in my blender. It was some kind of daiquiri, but Lizzie wouldn't tell us what was in it. I let the tangy fruit flavor melt on the tip of my tongue, trying to guess. Mint from my garden. The banana on my kitchen table. Lime. Rum. God knew what else. Whatever it was, Lizzie was a genius. The barbecue was lit and Bart had promised to make his specialty, *carne asada*. He'd even bought the groceries himself, and the kitchen looked like a tornado had blown through. But I didn't mind. The only thing I like better than doing the cooking myself is having someone else do it for me.

I took another sip of the daiquiri and asked Erica, "You think Hancock bought it?"

"God, he was eating it up. When I told him my pen name, he actually stuttered. Said his mom read my books all the time. When I told him I needed to know how a cop spent a typical day, the first thing he wanted to know was would his name be in the credits."

Bart was sitting up on his chaise lounge. "What pen name? You a writer?"

Erica told him who she was but Bart looked blank. Erica laughed, then saw the look on Lizzie's face. She'd flushed, and her big brown eyes had grown huge.

"You're Sheila Gay? No way! I can't believe it! I've read every single one of your books! I love them!" She was practically stammering.

"Thank you," Erica said, used to the reaction but clearly still embarrassed by it. "So anyway, the great deputy went out of his way to show me his daily routine. Even took me for a tour in the sheriff's boat, and I got to watch him issue citations for real exciting stuff like lapsed boat registrations and nonfunctioning fire extinguishers. Since Booker was off on other business, it was just the two of us and once I got him talking, there was no stopping him. To tell the truth, I think he has visions of himself as the hero in my next book."

Lizzie was still staring at Erica, shaking her head. Even Bart seemed impressed — by Lizzie's reaction, if nothing else.

"So? What did you find out?"

"Our hero likes to gamble. Sees himself as a high roller. Sees this deputy stint as more a learning experience than a lifetime vocation. Thinks Booker's a little uptight. Thinks Cedar Hills is totally backwoods. Says Oregon women are too fat for his liking, but very accommodating, if I know what he means. I kid you not. He winked at me as he said this, like I'm supposed to appreciate that. Anyway, I kept stoking the fire with little questions, just to keep him talking, and guess what I found out?" Her blue eyes were lit up with excitement and she leaned forward on her chaise lounge. "Guess where Deputy Dipshit plays cards every Friday night?"

"Professor Cathwaite's," Lizzie and I said simultaneously.

"Bingo. I asked what kind of cards and he turned real vague. I told him I loved to play poker and blackjack but that my favorite was Seven Card No Peekaboo. He said, 'See? We've got something in common. My favorite's called Seventh Heaven.' I told him I'd never heard of it and he said it was a new game, too complicated to explain. Then he turned on the siren and chased down a fisherman to check his license, and we never got back to the subject."

"Somehow, I don't think it's cards they're playing at the professor's," I said.

"What do you think it is, then?" Bart asked.

"Don't know exactly." I thought about the title of Cathwaite's dissertation — *Predicting Human Behavior: A Study in Probability and Personality Traits.* Probability was a term used by gamblers. Cathwaite studied human behavior. He videotaped complete strangers and their reactions to stimuli he controlled. And what? Predicted the outcome? Bet on it?

"Oh, shit." I said.

"What?" The three of them watched as I stood up and went to the railing of the deck.

"They're betting on human lives," I said. "I don't know the rules of the game, or what the stakes are, but that's what they're doing. I wonder which one of them is winning this one?"

"You mean you think someone bet that Buck would cheat us?" Bart said.

"Or that someone would attack Tommy?" Lizzie asked.

"I don't know. My guess is the attack on Tommy wasn't foreseen. Something went wrong. But can't you see it? They sit around watching the video, predicting the way the subjects will perform."

"Playing God," Erica said.

"Seventh Heaven," Lizzie said. "It's perverse."

"Yeah, but is it illegal?" Bart asked.

"I don't think there's a law against taking a picture of a stranger," Erica said. "You take your video cam to the beach and catch someone strolling by, you're not breaking the law, right?"

"Right. Lots of people use surveillance equipment," I said. "Convenience stores, banks, employers, insurance adjustors . . ."

"Private eyes," Erica chimed in, grinning at me.

"Exactly. It just depends on where and how you use it."

"What about invasion of privacy? The tape in my bar can't be legal," Lizzie said.

"Neither is what I have in mind," I said, grinning.

"What do you mean?" Bart asked.

"I'm thinking a little quid pro quo might be in order. Time to find out just how Seventh Heaven is played and who the players are."

"How do we do that?" Lizzie asked.

We spent the rest of that lovely evening working out the details.

Chapter Fourteen

Bart was the only one whose mission had yielded no results. After an entire day spent prowling the streets of Cedar Hills, he still hadn't seen a white car with a Triple A sticker on the bumper, nor had he seen any sign of Buck, who was presumably camping out on the ridge. He would've continued his search for the car on Thursday if he hadn't had to go back to work at the garage. I assured him that we'd know soon enough anyway, and told him to be ready for Friday. Meanwhile, Erica, Lizzie and I had our work cut out for us. Lizzie's job was twofold. She needed to let the Cathwaites know that she'd be doing the bartending at the party Sunday along with Kelly, and she needed to see if her sister-in-law could get me onto the catering crew. Meanwhile, Erica needed to persuade Newt to invite her to the party.

While they took care of business on their end, I worked on the technical details. I'd used taping and tracking devices in my line of work, but had never actually videotaped anyone using the kind of equipment we'd found in Lizzie's tavern. After several phone calls, I drove all the way to Eugene, bringing the video cam with me to a store called Boney's Cellar. It was a dingy little place tucked away on a side street, and though its brochure said it catered to law enforcement, I had the distinct impression Boney's real clientele ran more to the seamy side of the law.

"Good piece," the goateed man said, examining the camera. He was stick thin, in his forties, with dirty ash-blond hair that hung limply to his shoulders and a scar on his right cheek that looked like he'd been shot in the face. He walked with a slight limp and I'd have bet good money that Boney was a Vietnam vet. "You want this to be remote-activated, right?"

"Right. I just need the other parts that go with it."

"You lost them?" he asked, raising one pencil-thin eyebrow.

"Kind of."

"The thing is, if someone else still has the other parts, they can activate this, you know? So you're gonna have to change the settings. Don't know if I've got something compatible in stock or not." Boney ducked down under the counter, pushed a button that made a back panel swing open and disappeared behind it. I took the opportunity to browse the store. The only other customer was dressed in battle fatigues and smelled strongly of body odor. He was checking out a pair of night vision goggles that made him look like something out of a horror movie. I moved toward a less threatening aisle and scanned the shelves. There were all kinds of interesting devices — a stun gun designed to look like a cell phone, a knife that shot out of a wristwatch, a hollowed-out walking cane that doubled as a shotgun. I had trouble picturing myself using any of them. *The bad guy comes in and I decide the best thing to do is stun him so I say, "Just a second, I have to make a call on my cell phone"?* I was saved from further imaginings when Boney returned to the counter with a black and chrome box and a broad smile.

"Success!" he said. "It's not the exact match, but it's compatible. Watch. Here's what you do."

He showed me the basics — how to set the camera and monitor on the same frequency, how the camera was sound- and action-activated and how to connect the monitor to my VCR at home. "You can actually watch the action from the monitor itself, but it's pretty small, and if you want to hear sound, you'll need to use the VCR and hook up to your television."

He explained that the tape in the camera was continuous, retaping over itself at the end of its ninety-minute revolution. The monitor could be used to view the live action and/or record the events onto a blank videotape, making it possible to save the footage I wanted.

"You can set the mike for close or distant range, too. It's important to know which one you'll need. If you set it for close and then they move out of range, you won't be able to hear what anyone's saying. The most important aspect of this device is knowing where to place it. You want inside or out?"

"In," I said.

"The best is behind a two-way mirror, but you probably don't have one of those." He looked up, hopeful, but I shook my head. "Well, inside a stereo speaker is good. Ever hold speaker cloth up to your face? You can see through it pretty good, but of course no one would think to look through it, would they?"

"Probably not," I admitted. "But wouldn't the sound from the stereo drown out whatever you're taping?"

"If the music is turned up, yes, that could be a problem. But how often do people really have their stereos blaring? Usually not that often, especially if they're talking, which is generally when you want to tape, right? But let's say the music is turned on. You've still got the picture, right? At the very worst, you might have to do some lip-reading."

I nodded, wondering if there would be speakers in the Cathwaites' game room. I was positive that there was one room in the house where the gaming club convened for their weekly rendezvous. The trick was to find it, get inside, hide the video cam and get out without being detected. Too bad they didn't make something to make me invisible, I thought. If anyone would have such a thing, it would be Boney.

Several hundred dollars later, I managed to get out of the store with only a few more gadgets than I'd come for — a neat false-bottomed purse that would hide the camera nicely until it was needed, and four headset walkie-talkies that would be put to good use Friday night. On the drive back to Cedar Hills, I went over the plan, checking for loopholes, thinking up worst-case scenarios and concocting backup plans just in case.

That night Erica called me and gave me the latest. Newt had invited her out for Saturday night. She'd declined, of course, saying she was busy but available either Friday or Sunday. He said he was busy Friday but how would she like to join him Sunday afternoon for a party out on the lake?

"Good work," I said.

"If he tries to kiss me, I'm going to vomit. God, I can't believe I'm doing this."

"Think of Tommy," I said. "Speaking of which, did you see him today?"

"Just for a few minutes. No change, Cass. The nurse on duty wasn't very optimistic. At least there's no infection. I did run into someone else there, though."

I felt my pulse race a little, knowing instinctively whom she'd met, but I waited for her to say it.

"She looked good, Cass. Maggie told me to give you her best. I hope you don't mind, but I mentioned Bart and that he might be getting in touch with her. She was very receptive. I must say, she didn't act very surprised to see me."

Which made perfect sense, I thought. Maggie had always insisted that deep down I was still in love with Erica. But there was no point in mentioning that now. I changed the subject back to safer topics.

"Did you get in on the catering job for Sunday?" Erica asked.

"Lizzie's still working on it. The sister-in-law had to check with her partner. They'll let me know Saturday. Lizzie made me out to be this gourmet chef, I think. Told her sister-in-law I was the lead judge in the chowder contest, and stuff like that. Now they're going to expect me to cook. I just wanted to get in and serve a little food. Oh, well. At least Lizzie's in as the bartender. Bart still hanging out at your place?"

"Yeah. I think he's afraid to go home. He's feeling guilty about letting Buck stay up there looking for the gold, but part of him is enjoying the hell out of it. Talk about a love-hate relationship. I think he really is going to call Maggie, though. I told him I thought he should."

"I'm glad, Erica. Thanks. Any sign of whoever was following you?"

"No, but I can't help feeling like I'm being watched. Today when I got home, I had the weird feeling someone had been in here. Nothing seemed moved or anything, but I don't know. Maybe it's having Bart around. Actually, I'm glad he's here."

"Well, keep watching. Any sign of trouble at all, I want you to get your ass over here."

"Is that an invitation, Cass?"

I was glad Erica couldn't see my blush. "You know what I mean."

She sighed. "Unfortunately, I do. I don't suppose you'd want to come over here? Play cards with Bart and me?"

I laughed. "Thanks, but I'll pass. I've still got some details to iron out. See you tomorrow, though."

"Cass?"

"Yeah?"

"Sooner or later we're going to have to talk, you know."

I let the silence build, then sighed. "I know. Good-night, Erica."

I hung up the phone and closed my eyes, letting myself think back ever so briefly to the kiss, Erica's tender lips on mine, my whole body tingling, wanting her with every fiber of my being. It was still light out, so I walked down to the dock for some fresh air. Across the cove a boat bobbed on the quiet water, colorless on the dusk-colored lake. I'd taken my binoculars up to the house and it was too dark to see whether someone was fishing or just soaking up the last warmth of a sun-filled day. As I watched, the boat coughed to life, turned and chugged around the bend, out of sight. Had I scared them off? Or was I just being paranoid? The little hairs on my neck were sound asleep. Everything was all right. It was probably just a couple out necking in the cool of the evening. But then why did I have the vague, unsettled sensation that someone was watching me? I hurried back up to the house, locked the doors, pulled the blinds and did what any self-respecting private eye would do in that situation. I made brownies.

I could tell before I even opened my eyes Friday morning that the weather had changed. For one thing, my right ankle ached where I'd pulled some ligaments playing basketball in high school. Also, the bedroom was darker and I'd overslept. I peeked out through the mini-blinds confirming what I already knew. Rain was in the forecast. If it was raining, would they call off the card game that night? Or worse, Sunday's party? My mind raced, trying to think of how to proceed if our plans were ruined because of the weather.

As gloomy as it was outside, I felt buoyant. I found myself whistling in the kitchen as I made coffee, thinking of excuses to see Erica earlier than our planned rendezvous at the county dock. I could make cinnamon rolls and take them over for breakfast, I thought. It would be safe with Bart there. And the three of us could go over the plans one more time.

Still undecided, I whomped up the dough, then hurriedly showered and dressed while the rolls baked in the oven. They might not even be there, I thought, carrying the steaming buns in a basket down to my boat. Which was fine. I'd sit out in the middle of Rainbow Lake with the mist falling down around me and eat them myself, sipping from the Thermos of coffee I'd brought. In fact, by the time I got to Erica's place, I was almost convinced I should do just that. But I told myself I was a coward, secured my boat to her dock and hauled my goodies up the ramp before I could change my mind.

She answered the door in a white terry robe, loosely belted and sexy as hell.

"Where's Bart?" I asked, peeking over her shoulder.

"I think guilt got the better of him. He said he was going to go look for Buck. What's in the basket?"

"Uh, I thought you guys might want to go over the plans again. I brought sustenance." I was beginning to wish I hadn't come. Bart's absence made the whole thing different.

"You going to come in, or did you want to eat in the doorway?" Erica grinned. "It's okay, Cass. Honest."

I followed her into the living room, feeling awkward. "I can only stay a few minutes," I said, realizing I'd probably gotten Erica out of bed. "Wow. I like what you've done with the place. When did all this happen?"

"Little by little," she said. "Every time I come up here, I manage to make a few changes. Most of it I hired out last summer."

When Erica's uncle had died four years earlier, she'd bought the estate, but I hadn't been inside since she'd started remodeling. Right away, I could tell the changes suited her.

"You've opened it up. It seems airier."

"Got rid of those God-awful curtains. And I stripped the paint off these walls. The natural wood's much nicer, I think. Plus, I had that sliding glass door put in to the front deck."

"It looks great, Erica. Really. You could make a living doing this. Sorry if I woke you. I forgot you're a late sleeper."

"Wasn't sleeping, Cass. As a matter of fact, I was thinking about you."

"Oh."

"Don't look so worried. They were nice thoughts. This room is a really good place to think," she said. "You can see out to the lake and on a nice day the morning sun comes in through the east window. Even today it's not bad."

"That's great. Listen. I just wanted to drop off the basket. I guess I'll see you around six?" I turned to leave but Erica blocked my path. She must have seen the panic on my face. She held up both hands, lightly touching my shoulders.

"Please tell me what you're afraid of, Cass." Her voice was low and full of emotion.

"I . . . we've already done this, Erica. I may not be a genius, but I do catch on eventually."

"I hurt you," she said.

I felt my face getting hot. I nodded.

"And you hurt me. So we should be even."

"It's not a game, Erica."

"No, I never thought it was. Do you know why I left you, Cass? You scared me. *We* scared me. The intensity. It was all-consuming. I couldn't breathe, I was so happy. I was afraid I was drowning, losing myself, becoming something I'd never been. I ran away, Cass. But I came back, twice. Three times, counting now."

"You're timing was always bad," I said, feeling my heart pounding so hard I was afraid Erica could hear it.

"I know. But maybe the third time's a charm?"

I started to answer but she moved forward, stepping into my space, daring me to pull away. Her eyes were so blue, I thought, like deep water. And her perfume, faint and tantalizing, filled my senses. Before I knew what I was doing, Erica was in my arms.

"There's so much I want to say . . ." I said, caressing her back, pressing my lips to her neck.

"Shhh," she murmured. "Talk later." Her voice was husky, the way I remembered it. My lips found hers tentatively, touching softly at first, then giving way to the pent up passion. I slid my hand inside her nearly open robe and felt a sound escape from somewhere in the back of my throat. My hand cupped her breast and she shivered, then moaned. I moved down, kissing her throat, her collarbone, working my way to the taut, full nipples. When I took one into my mouth, Erica cried out.

The robe fell to the floor as I continued my descending exploration of the body I remembered so well. Her skin was smooth and warm, and I could hear her heart beating in cadence with my own. My fingers brushed the glossy black triangle of curls and Erica bit my shoulder, making a noise that both frightened and excited me. We were still standing, barely, on trembling legs. She'd never looked more beautiful, I thought.

"Please take me to bed, Cass," she whispered.

She didn't have to ask a second time.

Erica had never been a shy lover, but I wasn't prepared for the intensity of our love-making. How could it be this good, I kept asking myself, taking her again and again to the brink of ecstasy, not caring which of us came crashing down first or how many times.

"For someone afraid of heights . . ." I murmured, unable to finish the thought because Erica was taking me there again and I didn't want to stop her, couldn't have if I'd tried.

Later, with tears on her cheeks, Erica asked me why I was crying. I leaned up and kissed one of her tears away. "Same reason you are, I guess." We left it at that. We were past words. And we were too exhausted to talk anyway.

When we woke, it was mid-afternoon and the rain

was coming down softly outside the open window. Erica was gazing at me, as was Pepper, who'd crawled up onto the foot of the bed sometime during our nap.

"You are so beautiful," she said. "The best part is, you don't know it."

This made me blush and my insides turned to butter again. I reached for her, but she rolled off of the bed, giggling. "Forget it. I'm starving. I'll faint if you don't feed me."

So I got out of bed too and followed her through the house into the kitchen. Both of us were stark naked.

The coffee was still warm in the Thermos but the cinnamon buns were long cold. I fed her one anyway, and she licked the icing off of my fingers in a way that made me moan. We sipped coffee right out of the Thermos, passing it between us as we fed each other. Then Erica got playful with the icing, and the next thing I knew we were on the living room floor, making love again. It was slower this time, less frantic, but still sweet and wonderful. Only the chill in the air motivated our eventual trek to the shower.

"Me first," I said. "I don't trust you in here." But she got in with me anyway and we almost managed to shower together without turning it into another exercise in erotica. Almost.

Afterward, we had to towel ourselves off sitting down. Neither of us had the energy to stand.

"What time are we supposed to meet?" Erica asked lazily.

"Oh, shit! What time is it?"

The day had slipped away. It was already five o'clock. If we didn't hurry, we'd be late for our date at the county park. "I've got to get some things," I said.

"I'll meet you there!" I hurried down to the dock, which is to say I managed to walk without stumbling, and roared across the lake to my house, smiling like an idiot, my heart as full as the moon, as light as a sparrow.

Chapter Fifteen

We were all in our places for Stage One of Operation Get Even, as Bart had dubbed it. This step was far less dangerous than Sunday's would be, but important, because we needed to know how many players we were dealing with and who they were. Bart was stationed in the County Park parking lot dressed in green pants and shirt he'd bought at a garage sale that morning. At a distance, it looked like the usual garb for a Parks and Recreation worker. He had a push broom and was making a show of cleaning the sidewalks nearest the dock. His headset was obscured by the ski cap he wore, which looked out of place in the summer but hid his red hair. He'd tucked the ponytail up underneath the cap, but a few wisps had already fallen down and if anyone looked closely, they'd probably recognize him.

Lizzie was a block away at Gus's Marina, pretending to wash her car. Not the best ruse, given the weather, but it was all she could think of. It was a safe bet that Cathwaite would either pick up his club members in the party boat, or they'd drive out themselves. The best place to pick them up would be the county dock. If they had their own boats, they most likely moored them at the marina. It was Bart's and Lizzie's job to note the license plate numbers of anyone arriving between five and five-thirty and relay them to Erica via walkie-talkie. Erica was in my Seaswirl, halfway between the county dock and the marina, waiting to jot down the numbers.

I was down on the fishing pier across from the county dock, fishing pole in hand, dressed in a yellow hooded slicker. Despite the fact that the rain had stopped, the outfit was not out of place and it helped me conceal what I was really doing. Because there were other fisherman down there with me, my job would be difficult. I'd brought my best camera, a digital Sony with a zoom lens that could take a decent closeup from that distance. The camera had a swivel-tilt eyepiece that allowed me to focus without holding the camera to my eye. Even so, it was hard to conceal the camera from my fishing buddies on the pier.

Bart's voice came in a rushed whisper over the walkie-talkie, full of excitement. "Here comes one now. White sedan. Just a second, let me get around back.

Ooh, you guys are going to love this. Guess what? Triple A sticker on the left rear bumper!"

If Bart didn't calm down, he was going to blow his cover.

"Plate?" Erica whispered into the mike.

Bart excitedly read off the numbers, then repeated them more slowly. I could see the man but didn't recognize him. Dressed in shirtsleeves despite the weather, he had no-doubt been well-built in his youth, though some of the muscle was turning to extra weight around the middle. He moved like an athlete, though, his stride confident as he made his way down the ramp to the county dock. In the distance, I saw the Cathwaite's party boat rounding the bend. Good. The man would have to stand around and wait, giving me ample opportunity to get a good shot.

"I've got incoming!" Lizzie hissed over the walkie-talkie. Jeez, I thought. She sounded like we were about to get bombarded by missiles. "It's your lover-boy, Erica. Looks like he's got his own boat. Want me to get his plate?"

"Very funny," Erica whispered.

"We've already got his license number," I interrupted. "See what kind of boat he's driving if you can."

"Ten-four," she said, clearly enjoying her mission. A while later she came back on. "Dark blue ski boat. Big, loud outboard. Coming your way, Erica. You might want to lay low."

"Roger that, good buddy," Erica teased. But she took Lizzie's advice to heart, because she ducked down out of view as Hancock's boat roared past.

"Got another one!" Bart said, forgetting to whisper. He caught himself and lowered his voice. From my vantage point, he was doing a good job of imitating a park worker, though I doubt any parks employee had ever swept the walks with as much enthusiasm as he did. "Big black Caddy. Old dude inside. Oh, you guys are gonna love this one. I ought to strangle the s.o.b. It's the old geezer in the bar."

"You sure?" I asked, feeling the excitement.

"Positive. He's cleaned up real good, but it's him. Let me get the number."

As Bart moved around to the back of the Cadillac, the old man descended the ramp to the dock. Despite the flowing white hair and beard, his movements were that of a younger man. He seemed to be quite light on his feet and in fact rushed to help steady the party boat as it sidled up to the dock. I took several shots, wanting to get a good picture of the man who'd played such a central role in duping the boys.

"Now this is weird," Lizzie whispered. "Hang on a sec. I better move back." A few minutes passed before she came back on. "Hang on to your hats, ladies. No offense, Bart. We just stepped up a notch in company. Mr. Stickwell who runs the bank in town just boarded his cabin cruiser. Big fancy white thing coming your way, Erica. You don't suppose he's one of the players?"

I watched as the cabin cruiser passed by the fishing pier, then slowed at the opposite dock. I could see Stickwell waving at the men on the party boat before roaring off ahead of them.

"Bingo," I said. "Stickwell's definitely in."

"Who's driving the party boat?" Erica asked. She wasn't much farther from it than I was, but I had the better angle.

"Not the professor. Must be Guy Waddell." I took a few shots of the man I assumed to be the famed handyman/errand boy for the Cathwaites. As I did, he seemed to look right at me, cupping his hand over his brow to shield his eyes from the glare.

I reeled in, talking animatedly to the guy fishing a few feet down, and laughed as I recast my line. I took one more surreptitious peek at the opposite dock, but the party boat was already pulling away.

"That looks like a wrap," I said, getting into the lingo.

"Roger that," Bart said.

"All clear here," Lizzie concurred. "I'll be there in a jiffy."

"Ten-four," Erica said. She started up the Seaswirl and put-putted toward the county dock to pick us up.

"Do better if you use bait," the guy standing a few feet over said as I reeled in again.

"Yeah? I'll keep that in mind."

The four of us waited at my place for it to get dark. I took the disk from my camera and slipped it into my laptop. With the Photoshop software, I was able to manually enhance the photos to my liking, enlarge them and print them out. While they finished printing, I called Martha at home and left a message on her answering machine, asking her to call me when she got in. Meanwhile, Bart and Erica made omelettes with the leftover *carne asada* and we devoured them at the kitchen table. I tried not to look much at Erica, but it was no use. Her foot kept finding mine under the table, and besides, I liked looking at her.

About nine o'clock we piled into Erica's boat and motored over to Sturgeon Bay. Cathwaite had seen my boat yesterday, and any one of them could have noticed it again today anchored across from the county dock, so we took hers. Lizzie and Bart were both excited about the adventure and jabbered the whole way over, but as we rounded the bend leading into the cove, they fell silent. Erica cut the running lights and slowed to a crawl.

"Hug the far shore," I said unnecessarily. She was already headed in that direction. The party boat was tied to the dock, as were Hancock's and the banker's. The walkway was well-lit with colorful Malibu lights and Japanese lanterns hung from the eaves of the front deck. Inside, the blinds were pulled, but bright light shone through the taller windows. The upstairs was dark, though, except for one room on the west side, facing the rear of the cove. "Could be the room on top," I whispered. "Let's get as close to the shore over there as we can."

Erica eased the speedboat around the curve, then cut the engine. We were right on the edge of someone else's property, but no one appeared to be home. From where we were, we could almost see the west-facing upstairs window of Cathwaites' place.

"Can you guys put us on shore?" I asked Lizzie and Bart. They had the oars out, silently nudging us closer. When the bow hit ground, I stood up.

"Wait here," I said.

"Cass, if they see you, it could blow the whole thing."

"They won't. I just want to be sure."

I slipped the binoculars over my head and leaped onto the bank, sinking ankle-deep in mud.

"Hope those weren't your good shoes," Bart teased in a whisper.

"Shhh!" Lizzie and Erica both admonished.

I ignored them and scrambled up the bank, working my way through the brush toward the Cathwaites' estate. The adjoining property was thick with wild berries and skunk cabbage beneath large cedar trees. It made for good cover, but difficult travel. Suddenly I heard a noise behind me and froze. Very carefully, I turned and saw two large eyes staring back at me. An ear twitched, then another. Then, deciding I wasn't much of a threat, the deer went back to grazing.

My heart was beating harder now and I hurried up the small knoll that skirted Cathwaite's property. Suddenly, the house loomed in front of me, its low stucco fence not a hundred feet away. I froze, hearing my own breathing but listening for the sound of the dogs. Had they heard me? Would the breeze carry my scent their way? The longer I stayed there worrying about it, the worse it would get. I lifted the binoculars and used my elbows to prop myself up over the crest of the knoll. I could see the upstairs window clearly. But I was too low to make out anything except the ceiling and the top of a bookshelf. There was no way to see inside the room from my position. If only I could scale one of these trees, I thought, wishing I had Bart's tree climbing equipment with me.

I was about to retreat when a rectangle of light sprang open from the wall next to the window. A door! I watched as two figures emerged onto the balcony, the tips of their lit cigars glowing orange in the night sky. Slowly, I brought the binoculars back into position and zeroed in on the faces. The banker and Professor Cathwaite were laughing, their voices carrying over the water in deep, hearty tones. Behind them, through the open door, I could just make out the blue luminescent glow of a large-screen TV.

Knowing I had what I'd come for and not daring to stay any longer, I inched my way back down the hill until I was well out of their line of vision, then stood and ran. Just as I did, the dogs started a chorus of furious barking and I hoped to God they couldn't hurdle that stucco wall.

When I reached the boat, Erica was frantic. "Get in! They just turned on some kind of searchlight!"

I leaped in and ducked down below the dash. I was soaked from the wet earth. Bart and Lizzie pushed us away from shore, then ducked down in the back seat. Sure enough, a roving searchlight mounted to the boathouse threw a harsh yellow beam of light across the water in a lazy arc that was heading right for us.

"Gun it," I said.

Erica pushed the throttle forward and the little boat leaped out of the water with a roar, barely skimming the surface as we skirted the beam of light and raced out of the cove.

"Uh-oh," Bart said from the back. "I think we've got company."

I looked back over my shoulder and saw two distinct headlights giving chase.

"Jet Skis," I said. "Somebody must've been right down there on the dock when we took off. Turn down this arm," I said.

Erica made a sharp turn, sending a rooster tail of white spray behind us. "Pull up there and cut the engine."

She gave me a look like she really didn't need me telling her what to do, then killed the engine and let the boat glide toward shore. All four of us watched as the two Jet Skis flew past us in the main channel, their high-pitched whine sounding like enraged mosquitos.

"Close," Bart said. "Now what?"

"We get out and wait. If they double back and see the boat, at least they won't know who was in it."

"I think they know my boat, Cass. Newt walked me down to it, remember? And someone was following me."

"Well, if worse comes to worse, you can say someone stole it. Report it missing tomorrow morning. Right now, we better get up behind those trees and lay low." Thank God it was a cloudy night, I thought.

We were no sooner crouched behind the trees than the familiar whine of the Jet Skis returned, this time with their lights off. They were going slower, one on each side of the channel, searching the shoreline for our boat. The one closest to us paused at the inlet where we'd detoured, but it didn't turn in. We watched, holding our breath as the two wave-runners disappeared into the darkness, their annoying engines finally fading into silence.

We waited another ten minutes and were about to make a dash for it when suddenly the party boat rounded the same bend, headed back toward the county dock.

"We could be out here all night," Lizzie said, shivering. To make matters worse, it had started to drizzle again.

I still had the binoculars around my neck and lifted them, focusing on the party boat. "Cathwaite's driving this time, and he's got the same two passengers as on the way over. Guy must be on the Jet Ski."

"Who was on the other one, then?" Erica asked.

"Newt?" But no sooner had I said it than Newt's dark blue ski boat roared past, rocking the party boat in its wake. Not far behind him came the banker's cabin cruiser plowing through the dark water like a fishing trawler. Lizzie was counting aloud.

"Had to be Mrs. Cathwaite on the Jet Ski. Her and Guy."

"They could be sitting back there just waiting, figuring that once we see the others go by, we'll think we're in the clear." I said.

"Or they could be back at the house right now, drying off."

"Wish we were," Lizzie said.

By now the party boat was just a taillight in the distance.

"Oh, what the hell. If they see us, they see us. I'm cold."

We trailed back down to the boat and climbed in.

"You want to drive?" Erica asked.

"No, no. You're doing fine."

"Hmph," she said, giving me that look again. I kept my mouth shut while Erica inched the boat forward through the dark water. It was more difficult to see without running lights, but more difficult for them to see us that way, too. When we finally came to the familiar island marking the entrance to my cove, Bart let out a huge sigh. We were soaking wet by now and all more than a little tense.

"Think it's safe to speed up?" Erica asked.

"Do it!" I said. She gunned the speedboat across the rain-spattered surface and pulled up to my dock a minute later. We raced each other up the ramp, laughing like the imbeciles we probably were. It had been an unnecessary risk and could've blown the whole plan for Sunday. But at least now I knew which room I needed to break into, and more importantly, I had a pretty good idea where I was going to hide the camera. If stereo speaker cloth worked, I figured the screen covering the speakers on the big-screen television should work as well. A trip to the electronics outlet in Kings Harbor in the morning would tell me if I was right.

No one was in the mood to drive back across the lake, so I set Lizzie up in the guest room, Bart on the sofa and Erica in my room. No one seemed surprised by this last arrangement, including Panic and Gammon, who acted as if they'd been expecting it all along. By midnight we were all sleeping like babies.

Chapter Sixteen

Martha called Saturday morning when I was in the shower. She and Erica had a nice long chat and when Erica finally brought me the phone, Martha was chortling up a storm.

"I knew it!" she said, unable to contain her glee.

"You jump to conclusions," I said without conviction.

"Cassidy, you are such a lousy liar. Anyway, I approve. By the way, I told her if she hurt you again I'd break her arm."

"Martha!"

“I’m kidding, okay? But we did have a nice little talk. I think she’s in love, friend, so be careful. You doing okay?”

I cradled the phone against my shoulder, trying to dry my legs without dropping the phone. Finally, I gave up. “Actually, yeah. Better than okay.”

“Your message said you needed a favor?”

I told her about the license plates and that I wanted anything she could find on a local bank manager named Stickwell.

“This still about Tommy?”

“Yeah. It’s getting interesting.” I didn’t dare tell her what our plans were. Martha got nervous when my job took me past the edges of the law. I knew if I told her, she would try to talk me out of it.

“Seems like you’re into some heavy stuff, babe. Sheriff’s deputies and bank managers? You told Tom yet?”

“Soon. The thing is, I’m still not sure about Hancock. He’s a member of the professor’s gaming club, but that might not mean anything.”

“Why do I get the feeling you’re not telling me everything?”

“Because you’re suspicious by nature. How’s Tina?”

“You’re changing the subject, but she’s fine. Says she can’t wait for you and Erica to come over for dinner. How’s Tommy?”

We talked another few minutes, then I stuck my head out the door and asked Erica to bring me the license plate numbers. I was still dripping wet but pulled my terry robe around me when Erica came in. I read the numbers to Martha, who agreed to get back to me when she could. Erica smiled and locked the door.

"Your friends sure are protective of you," she said, playfully tugging at the robe I'd just belted.

"They know your reputation," I said, trying to ignore her. I turned on the blow dryer but it was difficult to concentrate with Erica nuzzling my neck, sliding her hands inside the robe, her fingers playing their way down my damp body.

"You're going to get all wet," I said, leaning back against her.

"I already am," she said.

And so began another glorious day.

Bart and Lizzie were long gone by the time we emerged. The plan was for them to take my boat to the marina where I could pick it up later when Erica dropped me off. I had an afternoon meeting with Lizzie's sister-in-law to go over the catering plans. Before that, I wanted to check out large-screen televisions in Kings Harbor. Erica said she'd go with me if I bought her lunch at a nice restaurant. Since the sun was shining again, we took her car, a new silver BMW convertible, and put the top down. Erica drove with one hand on the wheel, the other hand caressing mine, singing lustily along with Aretha Franklin. It felt good to have the sun beating down on us, our hair whipping in the wind, and I was almost disappointed when we pulled into the parking lot.

The sales clerk at TV Land thought I was nuts when I asked him to take the speaker cloth off the

56-inch television set on display so that I could see what it looked like behind it. I had to promise to buy the TV if we couldn't get it back on exactly right. Actually, it was attached to a rectangular frame and popped out easily. To my delight, there was plenty of room to set my video camera on top of the speaker behind the cloth. Better yet, when I held the black cloth to my face, I could see right through it, though from the front, it looked completely opaque. It was the perfect hiding place for surveillance equipment. By now the clerk was looking at me with real concern. I popped the speaker cloth frame back into place and thanked him, getting out before he called for the men in white coats.

"Feed me," Erica said, sliding into the passenger's side so I could drive.

"Seafood?"

"Perfect."

"Outside dining?"

"I'd eat in a damned cave. Just feed me."

Outside dining it was, at a little place I'd found called The Sea Urchin's, well off the beaten tourist path. Sitting on a prime costal lot, the tiny restaurant only had enough room inside for about six tables, so the owner had built a staircase to the roof, laid down AstroTurf, installed plexiglass around the perimeter to keep the ocean breezes from blowing anyone off the roof and now offered one of the nicest, albeit casual, ocean-view dining experiences in Oregon, made all the better for still being largely undiscovered. The tables and chairs were plastic, and when they brought the Maine lobster, they used newspapers to serve as table-cloths, and bowls of warm lemon water for our hands. The lobster was fresh and succulent, the crusty loaf of bread still warm, the Oregon Ale icy cold. We pulled hunks of bread from the loaf, dipping them into the melted butter, laughing at the sheer pleasure of eating like barbarians. Amazingly, we had the rooftop to ourselves that afternoon. The sun beat down on us, making the water just beyond the breaking waves seem golden.

"I don't want to leave," Erica said.

"They'll kick us out eventually," I said. "And I have to meet the caterer."

"No." She looked at me in a way that made my stomach somersault. "I mean, *leave* leave. The lake. Cedar Hills. You."

"Oh."

"That's it? 'Oh'?"

"Big Oh?"

She laughed, kicked me under the table. "Forgive me for expecting a little more enthusiasm."

"Forgive me for not showing it. It's there. Just beneath twenty layers of sheer terror, it's there."

She laughed again, but her eyes turned serious. "At least you're honest, Cass. About being terrified. I've known that about you for a long time. Big strong Cassidy James — scared shitless of falling in love."

"Is that what you think?"

"Isn't that what it is?"

We let the silence hang there. I wasn't sure anymore what I was afraid of. Something about caring too much, feeling too deeply. If I let myself really fall, I might not be able to get back up. If something happened to Erica, like it had to my first lover, Diane, I wasn't sure I'd survive.

"Hey," she said, taking my hand in both of hers. "We don't have to talk about this right now."

I nodded, not knowing how to say what I felt.

"Come on. Let's get out of here before they bring the dessert tray. I'm almost hungry again."

But try as she might to keep things light, I knew I'd cracked open a long-closed vault that sooner or later I was going to have to explore. I couldn't go the rest of my life afraid to live. Maggie Carradine had been right all along. I continued to fall for unobtainable women because they were safe. As long as I couldn't get too close, I wouldn't feel too much, which would keep me from being too devastated when they were gone.

But Erica wasn't unobtainable. She was right here, right now. And she was definitely not safe. Despite every warning going off in my head, I knew I wanted her right where she was.

With a peck on the cheek and a promise to call me later that night, Erica dropped me off in front of Lizzie's tavern, then sped off to visit Tommy. She'd sensed my need to think things through and without saying so, she was giving me space. Inside, the tavern was cool and dark. Lizzie's sister-in-law was sitting on a stool sipping iced tea.

"Sorry I'm late," I said.

She looked me up and down, appraising me coolly. She was a heavyset woman with flabby, dough-like arms that waggled when she shook my hand. "Call me Dora. Liz says you want to help out tomorrow?"

"If you can use me at all. I'll cook or clean or serve or chop and dice, whatever you need most." I sounded like a desperate out-of-work short-order cook.

We'd decided against the truth. The fewer people who knew, the better.

"Well, we could use an extra hand on cleanup. The food's pretty much all taken care of, plus you need a food handler's license for that. But when things pick up, it's hard to keep up with the dirty dishes. It won't pay much."

"That's okay," I said hurriedly. I gave her a pathetic, pleading look and she stood up.

"Okay then. We set up at eleven o'clock. Party starts at noon and we want everything in place when the first guest arrives. Lizzie says she can give you a ride."

"Great!" I said. "Thank you, Dora."

"Don't be late," she said. God help me, I thought, if I ever found myself in a subservient position where I had to kowtow to a boss. Here the lady had just done me a favor, and all I wanted to do was slug her. But I smiled gratefully and followed her to the door.

When she left, I went back in and ordered a beer.

"So everything's coming together," Lizzie said.

"Keep your fingers crossed."

"For you and Erica, too."

I looked at her over the top of my glass. Her big brown eyes were smiling. "Could hardly keep your hands off each other last night. Bet you couldn't wait for us to get outta there this morning."

"Lizzie! Don't be ridiculous!"

But her smile was even wider. "Always thought you two were cute together. When she dumped you, I felt real bad."

"She didn't dump me. Exactly."

"Well, anyway. It just feels right, her being back now. I still can't believe she's Sheila Gay! I'm gonna go back and read every one of them all over again, now that I know the author. You want me to pick you up tomorrow like I told Dora?"

"Yeah. It wouldn't hurt to have a different boat out there. They don't know me, but they might recognize my boat. See you tomorrow, Lizzie."

Feeling strangely emotional, I walked back out into the bright afternoon. Maybe it was the full moon on its way. Or too much sex. Or too much lobster. I couldn't put my finger on it, but I wanted simultaneously to shout with joy and throw myself on the ground and sob. I did neither. I headed to the marina, hopped in my boat and let the warm breeze comfort me all the way across Rainbow Lake toward home.

Chapter Seventeen

Sunday morning, I awoke with butterflies in my stomach and a kink in my neck. I'd slept fitfully, the sporadic dreams unsettling. In one, Erica and I were looking frantically for Tommy. Men on Jet Skis were chasing us and the whole thing was being videotaped by *Candid Camera*. Suddenly, Erica and I were in the water. I knew we had to reach the dock before the Jet Skis found us, but Erica kept pulling me back, trying to kiss me. We made love in the water forgetting all about the Jet Skis and suddenly they were right on top of us. "Help!" I yelled to the fisherman standing on the pier. Just before I woke, the fisherman looked down on us, scratching his beard. “Can’t catch ’em without bait,” he said, planting the seed for an idea that wouldn’t come to me until much later.

By the time Martha called, I was already up and through with my daily exercise program. I had even taken a swim in the lake, trying to work out the tension that still lingered. I was nervous about the plan, second-guessing the wisdom of breaking into a locked room with so many people around. I was sure the room would be locked. Maybe even had a tripwire. If so, I was dead meat.

“The first plate you gave me on the white sedan belongs to a Maxwell P. Hawkins,” Martha said. “Used to be a big-time college football coach back East. The Hawk. You might remember him. He got banned from the game for betting on his own team.”

“Like Pete Rose?”

“Exactly. Only this guy was betting *against* his team. Anyway, he moved out West and made it big in real estate. Now he’s fairly-well known around town. Clean as a whistle, too. Not even a traffic fine.”

“How about the second one? The black Caddy?” I asked.

“Belongs to a guy named Kip Cage, a professor at Kings Harbor Community College. In his late sixties. Again, no record. Great name, though.”

Kip Cage. The coauthor of Professor Cathwaite’s book. And the white-bearded con man who set Tommy up in the first place.

“What about the banker? Anything on him?”

“Stickwell? Another upstanding citizen. Sits on several boards, served as Grand Marshal of the

Veterans Day Parade a few years ago, like that. He did have a DUI several years ago but got the charges dropped somehow. The guy probably has all sorts of connections. These are the high and mighty, Cass. Whatever this club is you're looking into, it's got a pretty elite membership."

"Thanks, Mart."

"You're not going to do anything foolish, are you?"

"No," I lied.

"Cass?"

"Okay. Maybe a little foolish. But not, like, major foolish."

She laughed. "Why don't I feel better about this?"

I promised her I'd take care and hung up, wondering about the group who gathered once a week to play Seventh Heaven at the Cathwaites'. Bigwigs with a penchant for gambling? Rich, important men who liked to play God? Power-hungry Type-A personalities seeking a bigger thrill? I looked at the photos I'd taken, now taped to my wall, and tried to get a feel for what motivated these people. Regardless of the allure, I thought, their little game had cost Tommy, and somebody should have to pay.

I spent the rest of the morning getting ready. I practiced removing the camera from my bag, using duct tape to secure it in place, though I didn't have a big-screen TV to practice on. Finally, I packed the essentials in my false-bottomed purse, including my lock picks, the camera and my Colt forty-five, sifted through my closet for something to go with the Hawaiian theme of the party, then waited on the dock for Lizzie. She was right on time.

"Where's Kelly?" I asked, climbing in.

“Should already be there. I told her I might have to leave early so she caught a ride with the catering crew.”

“Nervous?” I asked on the way over.

“Hell yes. You?”

“A little,” I admitted. “You think Bart will come through?”

“The kid’s practically chomping at the bit. Said he always wanted to be an actor. Now’s his chance. You arrange for the Jet Ski?”

“Already paid the rental fee. All he has to do is pick it up at the marina.”

Lizzie was wearing a pink and yellow flowered scarf over her hair to hide her headset. It wasn’t quite Hawaiian, but would have to do. Actually, I thought it made her look like a little old lady, but I didn’t say so.

“Like your shirt,” she said, indicating the one Hawaiian shirt in my wardrobe. “How do you like the scarf?”

“Smashing,” I said.

“Liar!” We both laughed, which helped ease our nervousness a bit.

When we pulled up to the dock, Guy Waddell met us with a dolly. The party boat had already docked with the catering crew and the robust women were hauling tubs of food up by the armload.

“Hope that keg’s still cold,” Guy said. This was my first real look at him. Thin and wiry with a muscled jaw and slightly bow-legged stance, he wore a lei around his neck and white shorts that showed muscled legs with a thick mat of black hair. He hopped into the boat and single-handedly hefted the keg onto the dock. Not just wiry, I thought. Strong as an ox.

"I'll bring the rest up if you want to start setting up. Bar's on the deck." He gave me a cursory glance — clearly I wasn't worth a second look — and pushed the dolly up the ramp toward the house.

"Good luck," Lizzie whispered.

"You too," I said. With a sense of foreboding, I followed Guy up the ramp, scoping out the surroundings as I went. A band was setting up on the front lawn, the guitarist doing riffs that echoed across the water. Wearing an oversized Hawaiian mumu, Dora met me coming back through the front door and frowned at me like I was late.

"Oh, good. You can help unload. Come on, I'll show you."

So back I went and played pack mule for half an hour until the food, in all its abundance, was inside the house. The catering crew was setting up a buffet in the dining room, and the spread was lavish. Cold dishes floated inside huge bowls of ice while Bunson burners kept the hot dishes warm. The tables were adorned with carved open pineapples and clear crystal bowls filled with floating chrysanthemums. As I unpacked boxes, I had my first opportunity to study Ginny Cathwaite. She was a petite woman with a boyish build and dark glossy hair cut in a pageboy. She buzzed around like a bee, dipping her finger into dishes for a taste, rearranging flower arrangements, straightening furniture. She was a whirl of energy, an Energizer Bunny on hormones.

"I hope you didn't forget the caviar," she said, lifting lids off of dishes for a peek.

Dora stiffened. "On ice. Third tray over."

Mrs. Cathwaite marched over and inspected the caviar, again dipping a painted red nail into the bowl for a taste. Apparently, she had no qualms about spreading germs to her guests.

"Perfect," she declared. "Dora, you've done it again. Everything is absolutely perfect!" She beamed a red-lipsticked smile that radiated across the room. Dora and the other servers bowed their heads at the praise. This seemed to be expected.

From the kitchen, I watched Ginny buzz in and out of the other rooms, directing others as naturally as an orchestra conductor. She'd been called cute, pert, a cheerleader type, but I wasn't sure those were the adjectives I would've used. There was a toughness beneath her shiny exterior, an iron will that seemed to dare anyone to cross her. No one did, including her husband.

He came down the stairs, the handsome charismatic professor I remembered from the lecture hall. He and Ginny were dressed in matching white cotton pants and Hawaiian shirts. Hers was tied in a bow beneath her breasts, showing off her petite figure. When he entered the room, he playfully tugged at the lei around her neck and she hit him just as playfully, a show of domestic harmony for the hired help. They looked the part of the casually rich — just hosting a little get-together for seventy-five or so of their closest friends. The food alone had probably cost over a thousand dollars, I thought. What with the booze, the twenty or so fishing poles set up for the kids, the water toys and the band, this little *soiree* was going to set them back a pretty penny. Again I wondered where the Cathwaites got their money. Lizzie said that Ginny didn't work, and the last time I checked, a college prof at the community college level didn't earn more than seventy thousand, tops. I wondered if one of them had inherited the money. Or maybe they did something else on the side.

"They're here, darling," Ginny Cathwaite announced. I looked out and saw the party boat arriving with the first load of guests. It looked like Guy Waddell would be busy for the next hour chauffeuring those without their own boats to the party.

The music started up and soon the place was swarming. Outside, the professor got several barbecues going, doing the guy thing while his wife buzzed around playing hostess. Kids were leaping into the water off the dock while others tried to fish on the other side. A few Hawaiian-clad couples were already dancing on the deck near the band, and with the arrival of each new boatload, the crowd seemed to grow more boisterous. I didn't recognize many of the guests as locals. They must've been the professor's colleagues or people they knew in Kings Harbor. I winked at Lizzie hustling behind the bar, and she rolled her eyes at me like this was the last time she'd ever volunteer to do this! She and Kelly were swamped back there. The booze was flowing freely and the noise level grew proportionately. I went back inside and helped keep up with the escalating mess while I waited for Bart to arrive.

The upstairs had been roped off with a red sash, reminding me of the old movie theaters. But there were three bathrooms downstairs, a family room with a pool table and wet bar, a nice quiet living room with a sit-down view of the lake, and of course the dining room and kitchen. All of these rooms were being used by the guests as they ambled through the house oohing and ahhing over how nice everything was. Without Bart's distraction, there was no way I'd get upstairs unseen.

Just as I was starting to wonder whether they'd ever get there, Erica and Newt arrived. When I saw them, I did a double-take. Erica was wearing a green and blue Hawaiian shift that ended mid-thigh, showing off her long brown legs and well-defined arms. Heads turned as they made their way through the crowd, and Newt looked like the cat who'd just swallowed the canary. He had his hand on the small of her back, proudly propelling her toward the bar. She was doing her best to tolerate the possessive gesture, but I could tell it bothered her. She glanced at her watch and I did the same. It was still too soon.

I had wondered if the gaming club members would be in attendance and I was pleased to see that all but the professor's colleague Kip Cage were there. Stickwell had brought his wife and children, the latter of whom were raising holy hell jumping off the boathouse roof into the water. Hawk, the ex-football coach-turned-realtor was there with his wife, too. She was half his age, I guessed, watching the two of them dance. But even with his beautiful wife in his arms, he seemed to be checking out the other women in attendance. And I noticed Guy, finally able to relax and join the party, talking with Ginny Cathwaite. There was an intimacy in the way they stood together, and I wondered if Erica had been right about the two of them having an affair. But if so, the professor was either oblivious to the fact or didn't mind. He was holding court by the barbecues, and his audience was as enrapt as his students had been in the lecture hall.

Suddenly the sound of Bart's rented Jet Ski

rounded the tip of the cove. I glanced at the bar and found Erica, whose gaze met mine. Lizzie heard the sound too and immediately reached up to adjust the knob on her headset beneath the flowered scarf. Erica said something to Newt, no doubt excusing herself to use the ladies' room. I hurried inside and positioned myself near the stairs, waiting for Erica to join me.

"This is it," she whispered. "I hope it works."

Just then, Bart's familiar voice rose above the din outside. He sounded drunk, which was part of the plan. At first I couldn't make out the words, but then the band stopped and even the children quit screaming. Bart's voice pierced the sudden quiet like a gunshot. "Hey Professor Cathwaite! Did you know Guy Waddell is banging your wife?"

I could see Guy and Newt pushing their way toward the dock. Bart was still on his Jet Ski, cruising back and forth in front of the dock, just out of reach. He wore a bathing cap to conceal his red hair and he'd smeared Noxema over his freckled complexion, making him almost unrecognizable, but not quite. The people inside the house migrated toward the noise, some of them smiling, not sure this wasn't some kind of joke.

Guy said something I couldn't hear, and Bart laughed.

"You hear that, Professor?" Bart yelled, making sure the entire party could hear him. "He says Mrs. Cathwaite's not that great of a lay! But I don't know. I thought she was pretty good, myself!"

Now he had Cathwaite's attention, as well as everyone else's. Even the catering ladies had eased toward the front door to watch the disturbance.

"Go!" Erica whispered.

There were still quite a few people around, but their attention was riveted on the unfolding drama outside. I ducked under the red velvet cord and raced up the stairs, my heart pounding. When I hit the landing, I dug in my purse for the headphones and slipped them on. If either Erica or Lizzie saw someone coming, their warning might buy me some time.

There were more rooms than I'd counted on upstairs, but only one was locked. I slipped out my lock picks and fiddled with them, willing my hands to quit trembling. There were two locks, but even so I was inside in under a minute. I doubled-locked the door behind me, then went to work.

The room was larger than I'd imagined and had a great view of the back of the cove. The blinds were open, which meant anyone on that side of the property could see me. But luckily, the party was contained on the other side. Down below, I saw the dogs — two Dobermans chained to a pulley that allowed them plenty of running room without giving them access to the guests on the other side. Agitated by the noise coming from the dock, the dogs were straining on their leashes, their teeth bared.

Inside, seven leather swivel rocking chairs circled a mahogany table which was centered on a large rectangular Persian rug. The hardwood floor was polished to a sheen. A stone fireplace filled one corner opposite me, a wet bar to the left and the huge entertainment center filling the entire wall to my right. In the center of the room, near the table, an easel-style flip chart was perched on a tripod. I flipped a page and saw what must have been some kind of scorecard. It was complicated, with points awarded not only for events but also for frequency and intensity, whatever that meant. I didn't have time to study the chart, but at a glance, it looked like Hawk was ahead in the current game.

Half a dozen VCRs connected to monitors like the one I'd bought at Boney's, were stacked on the shelves of the entertainment center, and from the glow of lights I could tell they were set to pick up action, though currently all the screens were dark. I'd have loved to turn on the big set and seen what the professor had been taping, but there wasn't time. I crouched in front of the television and used a screwdriver to pry off the speaker cloth frame on the left. I set the camera so it would face the mahogany table, hoping I had the angle right, then taped it into position. I slid the frame back into place and patted it down, hoping that if they turned the TV on, the noise from the television itself wouldn't drown out the sound of their voices. If it did, we'd have to take a crash course in lip-reading, like Boney had suggested. As quickly as possible, I used the remote control to adjust the volume so that it came primarily from the right speaker, helping to reduce the chance of interference.

"Oh, oh," Lizzie's voice came over the wire, making me jump. "Bart's about to get his ass kicked. Can he go yet?"

"Go!" I said.

"Woo-hoo!" Bart's yell carried over from Lizzie's microphone, and I heard the Jet Ski roar off with the sound of two others right behind it.

"You out?" Lizzie asked.

"Not yet. Another minute."

"It's getting kind of crowded in here," Erica said.

"Ten-four."

I was opening the drawers and cabinets on the entertainment center, searching for Cathwaite's video collection. When I pushed in on a tall thin door, it popped open, revealing an impressive array of vertically stacked videos. The rack rotated with a push of a lever, and I found what I was looking for on the third rotation. Home videos with neatly penned titles on the outside of the boxes read *Fire in KH Diner, Scandal in Hawk's Church, Pizza Boy's Temptation* — the list went on and on. I was struck by the sheer number of them. How long had these guys been doing this?

"Trouble, Cass. The Cathwaites are coming up the stairs right now!"

I didn't have time to reply. I dumped several of the tapes into my purse, slipping the empty boxes back onto the shelf, then closed the cabinet door. I could hear their voices right outside the door.

The usually unflappable professor was in a rage. "Bullshit! Don't tell me you don't know who he is. It's the kid in the bar. The one whose brother is up on that ridge right now!"

"Do not raise your voice to me," she hissed. "I'm telling you, I've never seen him before. Now get back down there and try to make light of this, for God's sake. We're not going to let some drunk kid ruin our party!"

They were right outside the door and I stood frozen, afraid any movement would be heard. His voice strained, the professor was obviously struggling to get his emotion under control. "You're right, of course. We'll talk later. You go on ahead. I'll be down in a minute. I just want to check this out."

I heard his key in the lock and my pulse hammered. I searched the room frantically but there was nowhere to hide. The balcony! I rushed to the door, unlocked it and slipped outside just as the other door opened and the professor walked into the game room. I sunk to my knees, then lay flat on my stomach, hugging the balcony floor. I could hear him inside, opening the entertainment cabinet. Would he remember how he'd left it? Had I taken a tape he was looking for? I crawled forward, keeping close to the wall beneath the window. Below me, I heard the guttural, unmistakable growl of two enraged canines. Their black obsidian eyes glared up at me, but I had no choice. If Cathwaite discovered a tape missing, it might not take him long to notice the balcony door unlocked. If he stepped out onto the balcony, it would be all over.

I crawled to the far end of the balcony where a colorful nylon hammock was stretched between the corner post and the railing. I hadn't noticed it Friday night. I could just imagine Mrs. Cathwaite sprawled in the hammock, tanning her belly in privacy. Suddenly, I heard the inside door to the game room open again and Hawk's voice boom out heartily.

"Hell of a party, Professor. Too bad we didn't anticipate the bozo on the Jet Ski. Coulda made a bet or two, eh?"

I pressed myself against the wall and put my ear to the wood, praying that neither one of them would step out for a smoke.

"What are you talking about?" Cathwaite asked, irritated.

"Think about it," Hawk boomed. "We could've bet on how you'd react to the little turd or how Ginny would react. Would Guy beat the bastard to a bloody pulp? Would you?" He paused, then added, laughing, "Would Ginny?"

"What are you saying, Hawk? You planned this? You're pulling a game on me?"

Hawk laughed again, a big, full-throated guffaw. "Hell no, Professor. Not me. I'm just saying it would've made a good game, that's all. In retrospect, it would've been great. What are you doing up here, anyway?"

"I'm almost positive that the kid on that Jet Ski is one of those twins from the tavern. Here. Let's take a look."

The two quit talking and I strained to hear the voices coming over the videotape, but couldn't make them out. I needn't have bothered.

"That's him!" Hawk bellowed. "You're right. It's the redheaded bastard sitting next to the Green kid. What in the hell was he doing here?"

"That's what I intend to find out," Cathwaite said. "By now, Guy's probably beaten the kid to a bloody pulp."

Suddenly, Erica's frenzied voice crackled into my earpiece. "Cass, are you okay?"

I whispered back so softly I wasn't sure she'd be able to hear me. "I'll know in a minute. Tell Lizzie to let Kelly take over the bar and meet me where we were Friday night."

I turned off the headset and stuffed it into my purse. I couldn't risk making any more noise. I detached the nylon hammock from the railing and tested it for strength. It would have to do. I tried to calculate the distance between where I'd land and the end of the dogs' leashes. No matter what, it was going to be close. I heard the band begin to play again and welcomed the background noise. Maybe no one would hear the dogs if they started to bark.

Taking a quick look around, I hoisted myself onto the railing, wrapped the end of the hammock around my wrists and threw myself over, bracing myself for the impact if the nylon gave out.

It was like bungee jumping, I thought, except in addition to worrying about hitting the ground, I had the snarling dogs to avoid. The nylon dug into my wrists painfully, but to my relief, the rope held. I was still a few feet off the ground, dangling just beyond the dogs' reach. They'd given up the deep-throated growl and had begun to bark furiously. At any second, Cathwaite and Hawk could look out the window or step out onto the balcony and see me.

Holding my breath, I let go of the rope and dropped to the ground, rolling out of the path of the lunging dogs just in time. I leaped up and ran toward the stucco wall that surrounded the property. The dogs kept up with me, tugging at their leashes, which kept them just out of reach.

"Stop that!" I heard Cathwaite's voice boom across the yard as he opened the door to the balcony. I dodged behind a tree and stood stock-still, my chest heaving. I didn't think he'd seen me, but the dogs weren't giving up that easily and continued their frenzied barking. If one of the leashes gave, I was dog meat. Literally.

"Come here, Franny! Here Zoey! Come on, girls!"

Obviously a J.D. Salinger fan. "Good dogs," I crooned under my breath. "Go to papa."

Franny, or maybe it was Zoey, showed me her teeth.

Suddenly, a woman's voice cut through the yard and I knew Ginny Cathwaite was on the warpath.

"Franny! Zoey! You stop that ridiculous racket right now! Come here this instant!"

Cathwaite called down to her. "Maybe you should just let them off their leashes, let them run around a bit. That idiot got them all riled up."

"Are you all riled up?" she asked, switching to a baby voice as she got closer. "Are my little poopies upset?"

Oh, God, I thought. Please don't let them off their leashes. The dogs started to wag their stubby tails, unable to resist her crooning.

"Come on, that's my good girls." When the dogs didn't come running over, she lost her patience.

"Get over here right this instant!"

Whining like pups, their rear ends wiggling, the dogs trotted back toward their mistress. I remained plastered to the tree, willing myself invisible. One of them gave me a last, feeble bark, but by then Ginny Cathwaite had them by the collar and was leading them back to their doghouse, where she directed them to stay inside until further notice.

"Aren't you coming down?" I heard her call to her husband in yet another voice. She was back to the party hostess. "People are asking where you are."

"On my way," he said. "They catch up with that little punk yet?"

"They're not back yet. I hope they're beating the crap out of him as we speak." Then she did a scary thing. She giggled. It was a girlish sound, something that didn't sound quite right coming from her. Like she'd punched the wrong button by accident and let out one of her alternate personalties. Despite myself, I shivered. Something was definitely off with this woman. If she was the one running the show, I thought, it just got more dangerous.

I waited until I was sure they were both gone, then peeked around the edge of the tree to make sure the dogs were out of sight. Then, not daring to look back, I made a dash for the wall and propelled myself over it, hitting the ground on the other side so hard it knocked the breath out of me. I regained my composure, got my breathing under control, and worked my way around the back side of the cove, through the berry brambles and skunk cabbage. When I saw Lizzie's boat I nearly cried with relief. Erica helped me board, her usually unruffled features drawn with anxiety.

"What happened?" Lizzie asked, motoring away from shore.

"I thought you were going to give me some warning," I complained.

"They came storming inside and pushed right by me," Erica explained. "I couldn't say anything until they were past. We didn't count on that. You okay?"

"Yeah. Sorry. Didn't mean to jump on you. I just about wet my pants back there, is all. You think Bart's okay?"

"Last I heard," Lizzie said, "he was leading them on a merry chase toward the county dock. Having the time of his life, from the sound of it. Hopefully he's safe at home by now waiting for us to pick him up. You get the camera in place?"

I filled them in on the details, explaining what had happened.

"Look!" Lizzie said. "Newt and Guy must've lost their race with Bart. You better duck down, Erica, unless you want your boyfriend asking you questions about why you're leaving early." The two Jet Skis were headed right toward us, and Erica ducked down before Newt could see her. I ignored them, though I could feel their gaze on us. I wondered how long it would be before they started to put things together. Hopefully not before we did.

Chapter Eighteen

Bart helped me carry the TV and VCR from my bedroom and set them next to the ones already in the living room so we could watch the videos while keeping an eye on the Cathwaites' gaming room. The camera was both motion- and voice-activated, but after Cathwaite and Hawk had gone back down to the party, the screen had remained dark.

We spent two hours watching the videos and it was enough to convince us that the players of Seventh Heaven would stop at nothing. In one game, the ex-football coach, Hawk, had planted a rumor about the pastor of his church, and the club had bet on which of his deacons would be the first to confront the pastor with the rumor. It was a mean-spirited, malicious prank with no purpose other than providing the club with something to bet on. The banker had once left a bag of counterfeit money lying in the employees' lounge at the bank, then made a big show of leaving for the day. The club members had bet on which clerk would find it first and how he or she would react. Ginny Cathwaite had written anonymous notes to every member of the Cedar Hills Elementary School PTA board, telling them that one of their members was a child molester. The club members bet on how each board member would react, who would bring the subject up first and who would be the one most suspected by the others. I knew by the number of tapes I'd found in the professor's game room that these were only the tip of the iceberg.

"Hey, here they come!" Erica said, pointing to the other TV screen. Sure enough, Cathwaite and his very agitated wife, followed by the rest of the gaming club, filed into the room. I turned off the TV we'd been watching and turned up the volume on the other.

"I knew they'd have to meet!" I said, feeling triumphant.

"Shhh!" Lizzie said. "I want to hear this."

"She is one pissed-off broad," Bart said. "I mean woman."

We were watching the grainy but perfectly visible scene unfold around the mahogany table. Ginny Cathwaite was on a tirade and the others sitting around the table were looking duly chastised. The party was apparently over but the gaming club members had stayed behind to discuss Bart's party-crashing spectacle. Even the professor's white-haired colleague, Kip Cage, had arrived for the post-party session.

"Somebody please explain to me why one of those ridiculous twins is suddenly shouting malicious vulgarities about me at my party! How does he even know I exist? Something is wrong here, and the only explanation can be that someone in here has opened his big fat mouth."

"Calm down, Gin. No one's told anybody anything. Right?" Cathwaite said, looking at each of the men at the table.

"I'm telling you, I think it's that Trinidad woman," Newt said. "I still think the Green kid may have talked to her before he, um, passed out. And now this Bart is staying out at her place off and on. There's got to be a connection."

"I thought you said he never saw what hit him."

"He didn't. But that doesn't mean he didn't guess."

"Well, the camera you set up at her place hasn't done us much good, Newt. Except for pornographic purposes," the professor said, chuckling.

"Can't wait to see it," Newt said.

Erica looked stricken. "They bugged my house?"

"Oh, God," I said, understanding just who was in the porno video.

"Shhh!" Bart and Lizzie hissed.

"Well," Guy Waddell said. "We wouldn't even have to be discussing this if you hadn't overreacted, Newt. I still don't understand what in the hell you were thinking."

"I told you. The kid came up to me on Saturday night all threatening like and said he knew what I'd been up to and he wasn't going to let me get away with it. He said he had proof. I thought he meant us. The game. I blew him off the best I could and was going to get input from you guys on the best way to handle it, but then I saw him in the restroom on Sunday and took advantage of the opportunity." Newt leaned back in his chair and yawned.

"Well, at least that's one thing we've learned from taping Trinidad's place. He was talking about having taken a picture of your truck. That's all it was, Newt. He thought you and the brother were ripping him off," Cathwaite said.

Hawk let out a guffaw. "I'm still kicking your asses on that one! How many days has it been? Ooh doggie, am I rackin' 'em up on old Buckie boy. You folks is gonna be flat broke by the time that ol' boy gives up."

"I think it's time to wrap that game up," Ginny said. "It's getting too complicated."

"We should've called it quits on that one the second Newt whacked the Green kid," Stickwell, the banker, said. "I said so then and I still say so. Rules or no rules."

"Yeah, well. That's 'cause you picked the redheaded one to hold out the longest," Hawk said. "Something about redheads being stubborn, tenacious and fighters to the end, if I remember correctly. What you failed to realize, Stick, is that the bald kid's a redhead too."

"Let's take a vote," Guy said. He looked at the professor, then Ginny. Ginny nodded and the professor spoke up.

"All those in favor of stopping the Rainbow Ridge Gold Game, say aye."

Five voices chorused in the affirmative. Only Hawk and Kip Cage voted to keep the game going.

"So be it," Professor Cathwaite said. "Guy, get the camera off that mountain tomorrow. Make sure you didn't leave any damn red bandanas hanging around either."

"Aye-aye, Captain," Guy said, offering a mock salute to the professor.

A little dissention in the ranks? I wondered.

"So what do we do about this Bart nuisance?" Ginny asked. "Obviously he's figured something out or he wouldn't have come here today."

"Let's keep an eye on him. We've still got the camera at the Trinidad place, right?" Stickwell asked.

Cathwaite grinned. "Oh, yeah, right in the living room. You guys are going to enjoy what we picked up on that one. I'm thinking maybe there's a game here, but you guys will have to decide."

"The redhead's screwing the Trinidad woman?" Kip Cage asked.

"Not exactly," Cathwaite said, laughing. "You'll see."

He got up and came straight toward the television, leaning so close to the camera that we could see the hair follicles on his neck. Suddenly, a soft hissing sound came over the speakers and I realized he'd turned on one of the tapes. There were no voices, but I could make out the unmistakable sounds of love-making in the background.

"Hey, I know *her*!" Newt said, his voice slightly muffled beneath the sound coming from the tape. "She's friends with Booker. What the hell's going on?"

Cathwaite was still chuckling. "It seems you've got

competition, Newt. Your girlfriend must play it both ways."

"Turn it off, Cass. I cannot fucking believe this!" Erica was livid. I hit the remote control and the TV screen went blank. My cheeks were burning. Bart and Lizzie were both staring out at the lake, pretending they hadn't heard that last bit of audio. The silence in the room was deafening.

"Okay," I finally said, getting up to pace the living room. "Let's go outside."

They followed me onto the deck, Bart bringing up the rear. He had helped himself to the fridge and produced four Coronas, which he passed around. "We deserve this," he said. No one disagreed.

"I feel safer talking outdoors," I said.

"Newt Hancock's the one who attacked Tommy," Erica said, "and we can prove it."

"But would the tape be admissible in court?" Lizzie asked.

"That's iffy," I said. "Depends on the judge, and these guys are all connected. Damn, there's got to be a way to get him."

"Not just him," Bart said. "They're all in on it. It's like they didn't even care that Tommy might die."

"Couldn't even say his name," Erica said, her anger heating up.

"Did you see Newt yawn when he was talking about it?" I asked. "The guy's a sociopath. No conscience."

"They're all that way. Like the game is more important than the people's lives they're playing with," Erica said.

Bart nodded. "And the whole time, they're betting on who will do what and for how long — like we're their fucking pawns!"

"Too bad we can't turn the tables," Erica said.

"How?" Bart asked.

"Maybe we can beat them at their own game," I said. "In the professor's book, he talked about people being predictable, especially in their weaknesses. Once you know their weaknesses, he says, you can exploit them, make them behave in predictable patterns, thereby essentially controlling them."

"That's sick," Lizzie said.

"So?" Erica asked, watching me. I was pacing the deck, the idea taking on a life of its own.

"So. What's their weakness? As a group, I mean?"

"They're cretins," Lizzie offered.

"Yeah. What else?"

"Power. They like playing God, controlling others," Erica said.

"Greed," Bart said. "You asked one time what they all had in common and we came up with money. But it's more than that. They don't just have money. They like money. They want more."

"I don't think it's just the money, Bart. I think it's the winning. The game itself is a power trip — it makes fantasy football look like child's play. But playing the game isn't enough. They want to win! You saw the way Hawk's eyes lit up when he was talking about outguessing the others. More than anything else, they each have a compulsion to win."

"They want it all," Lizzie said. "I've seen gamblers

like that. They're up ten thousand and can't quit. By the end of the night they're down to nothing because they wanted more."

"So we've got to capitalize on their compulsion or greed or whatever it is," Erica said. "How do we do that?"

"I have an idea," I said. "But it's going to take Buck's help."

"Buck?" Bart's eyes were wide.

"Yep. And some good acting over at Erica's. Not to mention luck. Come on. Let's get to Rainbow Ridge before dark."

Chapter Nineteen

Buck was in no mood to be placated. He was tired to the point of exhaustion, having not come down from the ridge for several days. His food had run out and we caught him just as he was getting ready to call it quits.

"Got some stuff to tell you, bro," Bart said. "But there's a camera up here somewhere that might be able to see us. I'll explain later. Follow us."

Buck was too tired to argue and climbed into his truck, following us back to Lizzie's house, the safest place we could think of. Lizzie let him shower first, then cooked a frozen pizza, which we shared sitting on the floor of her living room.

"I don't fucking believe this," Buck said over and over as Bart told him the story. "How come you didn't tell me sooner!" He glared at his brother, looking ready to explode. His nose stud gleamed menacingly.

" 'Cause you were acting like an asshole, that's why." They stared at each other for half an eternity and I was afraid of what Buck might do.

Finally, Buck nodded and leaned back against Lizzie's sofa. "Okay. I've been an asshole. I apologize, okay? So why are you telling me now?"

"Because they're bigger assholes," Erica said. Bart laughed and Lizzie choked on her beer. Even Buck smiled. He almost looked like a nice guy for a minute, I thought. I sensed that underneath all that anger still lingered the sweet seven-year-old boy who'd held his little sister in his arms. But that little boy didn't stay out long.

Buck looked at me and scowled. "And why exactly is it you need me?"

"Because they're still watching you, for one thing," I said. "And it's kind of poetic justice. They've been using you and now you get to use them."

"By pretending to find the gold," he said.

"Right," Bart said, nodding. "You think they're going to let you keep it? No way! They'll come after you."

"Try to kill me, you mean."

"We won't let it get that far, Buck," I said.

"Hey, I ain't worried. I'm just trying to understand the plan." He pushed another piece of pizza into his mouth and chewed thoughtfully. He smiled again. "Tommy's got some burlap sacks in the garage that would probably do the job. You sure we have to do this tonight?"

"Guy's coming for the cameras tomorrow," I said. "If our part works, they'll be checking their monitors sometime tonight or tomorrow morning."

"What do you want me to do?" Lizzie asked.

"Stand by," I said. "You're our backup plan."

"How do you mean? What should I do?"

"Well, if we screw up and they get to Buck before we get to them, then they'll come after us next. If that happens, someone needs to tell Booker what happened."

"Oh, great. I get to be the bearer of bad news."

"Someone has to know what's going on, Lizzie. If you come with us over to Erica's then they'll know you're in on it too. All that does is put you on their list along with us. So far, they don't know you're involved."

"We think," she said. She looked up at the ceiling and raised her voice. "If you're listening, you sons of bitches, take this!" She raised her middle finger and saluted the overhead lamp. Bart followed suit, and soon all of us except Buck were flipping off the ceiling.

"This thing has really gotten to you guys, you know that? Jeez. And I thought I was stressed." Buck stood up, stretched, belched and made his way out of the living room, shaking his head.

"See you later, bro," Bart called.

"Later, dude."

Ten minutes later, Erica, Bart and I were skimming across the dark water toward Erica's, ready to act our part in the charade.

Erica and I had surreptitiously located the camera in her living room, hidden in a hanging basket behind a silk Boston fern. Making sure the camera would pick up the action, we positioned ourselves on the sofa, at a safe distance from each other, and pretended to watch TV. There was no way we were going to give a repeat performance of what they'd seen earlier. I knew that the minute we entered the room, the camera had started rolling. I just didn't know how long it would be before Cathwaite would check his monitor.

Bart knocked on the door and Erica went to let him in. I could tell by his eyes that his excitement wasn't completely feigned. Either that, or he'd missed his true calling.

"What the hell were you doing out there today, Bart? You practically ruined the whole party!" I said, following our rehearsed script.

"Oh, that. It was just an act, Cass. Newt Hancock paid me to do that, said it was some kind of joke he was playing on the professor. Something about betting on how he'd react. Paid me five hundred bucks, can you believe it? Easiest money I ever made."

"You're kidding! Five hundred dollars! I don't get it. What kind of joke is that?"

"I have no idea. Some sort of game. Anyway, that's small change compared to what Buck's got."

"Oh, come on. I don't want to hear any more

about that stupid lost gold. I'm telling you, the old man was pulling your leg."

"No, Cass! Listen. I went up on the ridge for a while to kind of hide out after my little prank at the professor's and I ran into Buck. He told me the notes were phony after all. He'd been going in circles and finally realized that someone was yanking his chain."

"So?"

"So, he's all ready to quit when suddenly he sees this big old elk go by and Buck thinks, hey, I never shot an elk before, so he goes back to the truck, gets his rifle and starts out after the elk. Only the thing takes him way the hell up this hill and down into a little valley where there's all this purple foxglove. And Buck's thinking about the first note where the guy talked about something purple, and so he's got that in the back of his mind while he's stalking this elk and then he sees it!"

"Another bandana?"

"No. The wagon! The actual wagon. I mean, he said it's all disintegrated and rotted through, but it's there. And the bags are totally worthless for carrying anything because they're disintegrated, too. But the gold is just fine. He says there's so much of it, it'll take him days to haul it out by himself. He offered to split it with me, if I'd help. Not fifty-fifty. Just ten percent. But shoot, it's better than nothing."

"You believe him?"

"He showed me one of the coins. They're Spanish, I think. I bit down on it and everything. I swear to you guys, it was real."

"So how come you're telling us, Bart? I mean, I doubt Buck would want us to know."

He grew silent, but his hands and feet continued to fidget. "Just in case," he said finally.

"In case what?"

"In case Buck doesn't keep his promise. In case something should happen to me out there."

We all paused, letting that sink in.

"You think he'd try to kill you? Your own brother?" I finally asked, incredulous.

"You don't know Buck. And it's a whole lot of gold, Cass. He says you can't even imagine it. Anyway, I'm gonna go up there tomorrow and see for myself. If I don't make it back, at least someone will know what happened."

"You want us to come with you?" Erica asked.

Bart laughed. "No way. Buck would kill me for sure if I brought someone else up there. He's the only living soul who knows where the gold is and he wants to keep it that way. I'll talk to you in a couple of days. Hopefully by then, I'll be a whole lot richer."

When he left, Erica let out a gargantuan sigh. "I don't trust that Buck as far as I could throw him," she said, speaking clearly for the microphone. "What do you want to bet he's making this whole thing up to fool Bart?"

"I guess we'll know in a few days. Bart will either be rich or heartbroken."

"Or dead," she said.

"Yeah, or that. Come on. Let's go to bed."

We made a big show of turning out lights, then snuck out of the house and hurried back to my place to check the action at the Cathwaites'. We wanted to know it the moment someone decided to check the camera hidden at Erica's. But the Cathwaite's game room was dark and silent, so we turned the volume up on my television and fell asleep in the living room, hoping the sound of voices in Cathwaite's game room would wake us. If no one checked, we knew we had just put on our little show for nothing.

But early the next morning, just as I was getting ready to shower, Professor Cathwaite came through. Erica heard the noise first and called me to come quickly.

"He's checking the monitors!" she said. Using a remote, Cathwaite clicked on one VCR after another, keeping tabs on the various games in session. We could not see the big-screen television — as our camera was hidden beneath the TV — but when the sound of Bart's voice came over the speaker, Erica shouted "Yes!"

"He's falling for it," I said, keeping my fingers crossed. We watched as Cathwaite rewound the tape to the beginning and replayed the whole scene. Then he stuck his head out the door and yelled for Ginny and Guy to get in there.

"I think Newt's about to get in big trouble," I said.

"What are you screaming about?" Ginny Cathwaite demanded, coming in wearing a chenille robe, her short hair still wet from the shower.

"Something you need to see. Where's Guy?"

"How should I know?"

"Right behind you, brother-in-law. What's up?"

"Guy's her brother?" Erica asked.

I shrugged, not wanting to talk over their voices.

"Listen to this," Cathwaite said, using the remote. Suddenly, our voices filled the speaker. It was eerie, I thought. We were watching them on my TV as they watched a tape of us on theirs. When it got to the part where Bart said Newt had paid him to play a joke on the professor, Ginny went livid, but the professor hissed at her to be quiet until the tape was over. When Bart made his exit, Cathwaite used the remote to stop the tape.

"That miserable fucking pig!" she spit. "He's not only a fuckup, he's fucking with us!" She was talking, of course, about Newt.

"It doesn't make sense," Guy said. "Why would Newt bet on us?"

The professor was shaking his head. "Should've seen it coming. We need to call a meeting."

"Now? On a Monday morning? What about work?"

"Right now. I don't give a damn about anyone's work schedule. Make it for ten o'clock. Mandatory."

"And invite Newt?"

"By all means. Definitely invite Newt."

"What about the gold? You think Buck really found something?"

"That's why we're calling the meeting. We'll deal with that pissant, Newt, later."

"Hot damn!" I said, dancing around the living room like a kid. I raced to the phone and called Bart.

"We're on!" I said.

"Yes!" he shouted into the receiver. "Buck, we're on! Let's go!"

Then I made another phone call, one I'd been dreading. Rosie answered the phone, then put Booker on.

"I'm not talking to you," he said.

"Don't blame you. But you're gonna want to kiss my feet by the time this day is over."

"I doubt it. Why?"

"If I asked you to do something really weird, I

mean really really weird, and I asked you to trust me that it would work out, would you do it?"

"Hell no. I can't even trust you to be straight with me! Sending me off on a wild goose chase while you and Erica work behind my back. You think I don't know you're up to something?"

"Tom. I would never hold something back from you unless I had a really good reason."

"Like what?"

"Are you sitting down?" I waited, knowing Booker was fuming. I took a deep breath and let it out. "Like your deputy being the one who tried to kill Tommy," I finally blurted.

"What? Newt?"

I didn't answer right away. I just let it sink in.

"You better talk to me, girl."

"I'm gonna let Newt explain it himself. But not right this second. First you gotta do me this one favor. I've got a list of people I'd like to call, on your behalf, and invite over to the town hall today at noon. I'd like your permission to say that there's a matter of grave concern and everyone should be there."

"How many people on this list, Cass?"

"Quite a few. A lot, actually. If they all come, we'll fill the place."

"And I suppose Newt's going to be at this meeting you're calling on my behalf?"

"Oh, yeah. Newt and some of his nearest and dearest friends."

It took me another half-hour to convince Booker. I ended up having to tell him everything and when I did, he understood why I needed to attempt this in public. He didn't like it. He called me unflattering names. But in the end, he agreed to phone a few of the more important ones himself and wished me luck with the others. I told him to hold off on calling the gaming club members until just before noon. I wanted to make sure they had their appointment at the Cathwaites' before they got the call.

Erica stood guard over the television, watching for any movement at the Cathwaites' and looking up numbers for me while I made the calls. After the first few, I had my spiel down to an art. I told them just enough to pique their curiosity, knowing they'd come for that if for no other reason. I'd picked noon because I figured those with traditional jobs could break away on their lunch hour. When the banker's wife told me she didn't think she could make it, I told her if she didn't she'd probably have to wait for the recap on the news that night. That got her attention and she vowed to change her hair appointment if she could.

The pastor at Hawk's church was another reluctant participant, but I promised him he'd never regret it. The Cedar Hills PTA board had no idea why they were being invited, but they all accepted. I invited Mrs. Peters, the town librarian, and Tommy's mother and aunt, Gus Townsend, the mailman, just about everyone I could think of who might care. Even the dean of Kings Harbor Community College said he'd try to make it, when I told him it concerned two of his faculty members. I called Martha last and was surprised to find that she was expecting my call.

"Booker told me," she said. "You really think this is going to work?"

Truthfully, I wasn't sure and told her so.

She chuckled. "That's what I love about you, kiddo. You convince everyone else that you've got the whole thing under control, when the whole time you're doubting yourself. God, I'd hate to see how dangerous you'd be if you ever believed in yourself."

"I don't have time for a lecture, Martha. Will you be there?"

"Are you kidding? You think I'd miss the Cassidy James version of *Candid Camera*? Of course I'll be there. With bells on."

"Skip the bells, Mart. Just bring your gun."

"I'll be there, babe. You just watch out for yourself."

By the time I'd finished talking, my ear felt like it would fall off, but the town was buzzing with anticipation over the unprecedented noon meeting. Erica was standing in front of the television watching the Cathwaite's game room. "They're all there," she said, waving me over. "They've been watching the camera on Rainbow Ridge for the last half-hour and from what I can tell, Buck just came into view, hauling empty sacks up the road. They're definitely buying this, babe." I liked the way that sounded. *Babe.* I smiled at Erica, knowing there'd be time later to tell her how I felt. I checked the tape twice to make sure it was working properly and sat back to watch the gaming club's final meeting.

Chapter Twenty

Not only had the people we'd called shown up, but quite a few we hadn't invited apparently heard about the meeting and came, too. It had been a rush to get everything set up and I was so nervous, my stomach was growling.

"I told you we should've eaten something," Erica teased.

"Later," I said. "You can take me to the Sea Urchin's and feed me Maine lobster."

"That's not where I'm taking you first," she said, giving me that smile that made my heart melt.

Booker came over, looking more nervous than I was. "Haven't seen the professor yet," he said.

"They just came in. I'm afraid they might bolt when they figure out what's happening."

"I'll be standing by the door. Anyone trying to bolt has to get past me. I just hope Newt doesn't try something stupid."

"Actually, that's what I'm counting on. Speak of the devil," I said, pointing my chin toward the back of the room.

Newt sauntered in, looked around the room with sleepy eyes until he spotted Booker, then walked over. "Hey, Sheriff. What's up? You got the whole damn town riled up. There gonna be a war or something? Someone drop a bomb? Maybe a meteor heading right for Cedar Hills? I'm surprised you didn't invite the media."

Actually, we had. But they'd promised to lay low until we gave them the signal.

"Something like that," Booker said. "Have a seat, Newt. I may need you later, so stick around."

"Whatever." He shrugged, straightened the brim of his Stetson and took a seat in the back of the room.

"Well, I guess this is it, then," Booker said. "I counted seven."

"Same here. Let's do it."

We walked together to the podium and Booker called the meeting to order. Just then, the door opened and Bart and Buck Bailey slipped in with Lizzie Thompson, joining Erica against the back wall.

"I want to thank all of you for coming out on such short notice. I know there's a lot of concern about what this is all about. I'm going to let my friend Cassidy James here explain it to you. I just ask that everyone remain seated until we're finished, and then, if there's any questions, we'll take them at that time. Cass?"

I moved to the mike and cleared my throat. "I was afraid someone might try to stop me from finishing, so I hope you don't mind, but I taped what I wanted to say. I hope you won't let anyone stop you from seeing it through to the end." I turned on the VCR and the two televisions in the front of the room came on, showing me in closeup. My voice sounded funny to me, and I could tell I'd been nervous during the taping. I moved to the side of the room and watched the gathered crowd as they listened to my speech.

"As some of you know, someone tried to kill my friend Tommy Green at the county park last Sunday. Tommy's still in a coma and the person who tried to kill him is sitting in this room."

I'd expected gasps of alarm, but the room grew totally silent. I watched Newt's blank expression for some sign that he knew he was in trouble but I had to give him credit. His face was a mask of calm.

"In the last few days I've learned some things that I find both shocking and repugnant. Some of you in this room have been the unwitting victims of harassment. You don't know it though, because the people doing this get their jollies from spying on you in places you think are private. They're not just spying, though. They're setting you up. Have you ever found money just lying around and wondered what you should do with it?" I glanced over at the bank clerk who'd taken Stickwell's bait. She wasn't the only one glued to what I was saying. "How would you feel, knowing that the money had been left there on purpose and that a group of people were betting on what you'd do with it?"

I watched Stickwell squirm in his chair, and he glanced over at Hawk who was sitting a few feet away. Hawk gave a slight shrug, then looked over his shoulder at the Cathwaites, but the video went right on.

"Ever have someone spread vicious rumors about you or a colleague? Bet you didn't know that the people who started the rumor were also betting on how you'd handle yourself. These people have set a fire in a public place just so they could bet on whether the victims would respond bravely or with cowardice. All in fun, mind you. Just a friendly little game among pals. Except innocent people have been getting hurt. And now one of them may die. Well, more than one. But let me show you what I mean."

The screen went blank for a second and I took the opportunity to study the players. Guy Waddell had stood up and was moving to the back of the room. Hawk, too, was on the edge of his seat. Suddenly the camera zoomed in on the Cathwaites' gaming room. Ginny Cathwaite let out a tiny gasp. They were all there, the seven of them sitting around the mahogany table. I'd edited it as best I could, keeping only what was pertinent. I glanced at the professor, whose face had gone deathly pale. Beside him, Ginny looked ready to kill, but neither one moved. Their gazes were glued to the television like everyone else's.

Suddenly, Stickwell leaped to his feet. "Now just a minute!" he bellowed. "You turn that idiotic machine off! I've heard just about enough of this nonsense!"

"Be quiet!" someone hissed.

"Sit down and shut up!" someone else snarled.

"Yes, sit down," Stickwell's wife said. "I want to hear this." To my amazement, Stickwell slunk back down in his chair and stared at the screen. Cathwaite had started to get up too, but Booker tapped his holster and shook his head, a silent warning that made the professor sit back down and watch the unfolding scene in his gaming room with everyone else.

"You think it's possible the kid really found the gold?" Kip Cage was asking on-screen, stroking his white beard. He chuckled. "I'll be damned. This game gets better and better."

"They're going up there tomorrow," Guy said.

"Maybe we can beat them up there, take it ourselves," Stickwell said.

"We don't know how to find it," Cathwaite said. "We'll have to let Buck lead us to it."

"And do what with Buck?" Newt Hancock asked. "He's not exactly going to invite us to share the wealth."

"Do what you do best, Newt. Same thing you did to the Green kid." Ginny Cathwaite's voice was laced with sarcasm. She could barely contain her anger over Newt's supposed deception.

"Shit. I don't have to put up with that," Newt said, pushing back his chair.

"Sit down, Newt," Cathwaite said. "What my lovely wife means is, if it comes to that, you'd be the best one for the job."

"What with your experience," Guy threw in.

"You all don't let up, do you? I told you. I did it to protect us. He was onto the game."

"You *thought* he was onto the game. He wasn't onto shit!" Ginny said.

"Now, now," the professor cooed. "Let's all just simmer down. The thing is, does anyone see a way of getting at this gold without taking the punk out?"

"What about the brother? The redhead?" Kip Cage asked. "And those two gals?"

Originally the line had been "those two gals we so enjoyed watching last night," but I'd cut that part out.

"Those two already think that Buckie boy might off his brother. If they both end up dead, it'll just look like a little sibling rivalry ended in a shootout."

"But won't they wonder where the gold is?" Hawk asked, chomping on an unlit cigar.

"So, let them wonder. One of them's already convinced that Buck's just putting his brother on. Maybe he was and the redhead gets ticked, pulls his gun and bang! They off each other!"

The professor was nodding. "I can see that. But it will take at least two of us to do the shooting. Then, more to carry the load down. You saw the sacks. There must be a truckload of gold up there."

"I'll go," Ginny Cathwaite said. "Me and Newt. We're the best shots, anyway."

Her husband looked at her, then nodded. "That okay with you, Newt?"

"Yeah. What the hell? We splitting it even, seven ways? Or do me and Ginny get a bigger share?"

"What's fair?" Cathwaite asked the table. Stickwell took out his calculator and punched numbers.

"It would help if we knew how much there was."

I'd fast-forwarded through the next part because they got long-winded, worrying over percentages.

When they came back on, only Cathwaite, his wife and Guy were in the room.

"You're gonna take out Newt, aren't you?" Guy asked. "That's why you volunteered."

"Unless you want to do it, Guy," Ginny said. "I was afraid you'd chicken out. He's gotta go. Don't tell me you don't agree."

"Oh, no. I definitely agree. You sure you can handle it?"

"I handled dear old Daddy, didn't I?"

And that was the end of the tape. I hit the off button and Booker turned on the lights in the back of the room, making people blink. Newt was on his feet, as were both Cathwaites and Guy. The banker, Cage and Hawk were still seated, but the people closest to them were staring at them, aghast.

Booker's voice broke the deafening silence. "Guess you owe Cassidy a big ol' thank you, Newt. Looks like she just saved your sorry little life."

Newt, for the first time since I'd met him, looked fully awake. His eyes darted from Booker to the Cathwaites, figuring the odds.

"You bitch!" I heard someone yell. It was one of the PTA women. She had climbed onto her chair and was pointing at Ginny Cathwaite. Before anyone could stop her, she took off her shoe and hurled it at Ginny, hitting her squarely on the nose which trickled blood. Ginny clutched her nose, her eyes suddenly rabid.

"You stupid bastard," she hissed, taking a step toward Newt.

“Me? I didn’t do anything!”

“You’ve ruined everything!” Before her husband could restrain her, Ginny Cathwaite lunged at Newt, raking her red fingernails down his cheek and throat, drawing blood. Moving quicker than I thought he was capable of, Newt backhanded her, sending her sprawling across the floor. By now, the whole room was in chaos, the crowd on its feet, moving away from the action, eyeing those in the fray.

“Don’t you ever touch her!” Guy shouted, slamming his fist into Newt’s gut.

Newt doubled over, gasping for breath. “What the fuck! This isn’t my fault!”

“Sure it is,” Cathwaite said, struggling to keep Ginny from rushing Newt again. “If it wasn’t for you, Newt, we wouldn’t be here.”

“Bullshit! She’s the one who wanted to kill Buck. And me! You heard them,” he said, trying a last-minute appeal on Booker, who still stood with his back to the door, his right hand hovering near his holster. Newt’s usually sleepy eyes were frantic.

“Yep. I sure did,” Booker said. “Heard you attacked Tommy Green, too.”

Newt’s eyes widened, like those of a cornered animal. Then he did something I had dreaded. He pulled his gun.

“What? You’re gonna shoot me, Newt?” Booker asked, blocking the door.

“If I have to, Tom. These guys have framed me and I’m not takin’ the fall for them. Now move aside.”

“You walk out that door with a drawn gun and there’s gonna be bloodshed, Newt. A half-dozen of

Kings Harbor's finest are waiting right outside the door."

"Nice try, Tom. You should know that as a gambler, I don't bluff easy," he said, starting to pace.

"He's telling the truth, Sheriff," Cathwaite said. "He'd just as soon kill you as not. I'm afraid your deputy's a good old-fashioned sociopath. We should've seen it sooner. None of us would be here if we had."

"No way!" Newt said, swinging the gun around to point at Cathwaite. "You're not going to stand there and pin everything on me. You guys were pulling this shit before I ever came along! It wasn't me who started those fires. That was Hawk! And Stickwell's little bribery episodes, proving which men's wives would screw him for money! Tell me that wasn't crossing the line, Professor."

"Shut up, Newt." The usual spark in Cathwaite's eyes had gone dead. By now, all seven members of the gaming club looked stricken. The others in the room had moved all the way to the front of the room, away from Newt's gun. Only the Bailey boys, Lizzie and Erica were trapped in the back, standing near Booker.

Newt waved the gun in their direction, then turned his attention back to Cathwaite, his tone suddenly sarcastic. "And your lovely wife, Professor. I bet the file's still open on her dear old missing daddy! Bet her little brother could tell us where the parts are buried, couldn't you, Guy? But you don't mind living with a couple of murderers, huh, Professor? As long as you get to enjoy the inheritance?"

"Get him!" Ginny screamed. I wasn't sure if this was directed at Guy or Cathwaite. Both of them stood stock-still, their faces mottled with anger as Newt's gun wavered between the gaming club members.

"Time to put down the gun, Newt," Booker said. Hancock looked around the room frantically. "Too many witnesses," Booker said, reading his mind. "You can't kill us all."

Slowly, Newt's shoulders slumped and he turned the gun in his hand so that the butt faced outward, then held it out for Booker. Booker stepped forward to retrieve it, and as he did, Newt made a sound in the back of his throat, kicked out at Booker's gun hand, then wheeled around and pointed his gun right at Erica.

"They're not gonna shoot me, long as I can shoot you first, right?" He pulled her against him and pressed the barrel to her temple.

"Don't do this, Newt. You're in enough trouble as it is," Booker said. He clutched his right hand but managed to mask the pain from his voice.

"That's kind of the point, ain't it, Sheriff? Come on, darlin'. You and me are going for a ride."

He opened the door and looked straight into the face of my best friend, Martha Harper. Behind her stood half a dozen uniformed cops. Their guns were drawn, but when they saw the gun to Erica's head, nobody moved. Beyond the line of cops, several media vans were parked, their video cams and microphones pointed right at Newt.

Newt blinked at the cameras, momentarily shaken before he regained his composure. "Put 'em away, boys. Uh, you too, ma'am. I know you don't want to make me have to shoot her."

Slowly, one by one, the officers holstered their guns and my stomach lurched. I couldn't believe that things had gotten so out of hand. And now Erica was in the middle of it! Suddenly, there was a blur beside me and before I knew what was happening, Buck Bailey was hurtling across the room, his body slamming into Newt's with such force that the floor shook when they landed.

"Let her go!" he shouted over and over, pummeling Newt with his fists, landing furious blows to the face and chest. Newt, whose gun had skittered across the floor, was no match for Buck's fury. He held his hands up to ward off the blows until Booker, Martha and another cop finally managed to pull Buck away. Erica, who'd been knocked down, got shakily to her feet.

"You have the right to remain silent," Martha said, hooking the handcuffs onto Newt's wrists. The uniformed cops filed into the room and approached the other six players warily, their guns drawn. Behind them, the news crews crowded into the room.

"It was just a game!" Hawk pleaded to no one in particular as the cops approached him. One of them stepped forward and showed him the metal handcuffs.

"Yeah? Well, it looks like you lost, ass-bite."

"What am I being charged with? I demand to know the charges!" the banker insisted, though his tone didn't hold much conviction.

"How about conspiracy to commit murder, for starters?" Martha said. "We've got at least fifty people, not to mention eight police officers and two news stations that just heard you jokers conspire to murder Buck Bailey. And I've got a feeling we'll be able to add to those charges real soon."

"Yeah!" one of the PTA ladies yelled from across the room. "How about conspiracy to ruin a person's life!"

There was a shocked pause, then someone started to clap. It was a strange reaction, I thought, but the next thing I knew, everyone had joined in, applauding in a steadily increasing cadence until the room sounded like a football stadium. I looked back at them, and realized they were clapping for Buck.

We watched the seven of them being led away, the camera crews getting it all on tape. Erica took my hand.

"We did it!" she said.

"Buck did it," Bart said, smiling at his brother who was still splattered with Newt's blood. He had an odd look on his face, almost peaceful, I thought.

"That was kind of close," I said. "But thanks."

"Hey. The dude's an asshole." He smiled at Erica and I recognized the look. It was the same one the seven-year-old in the picture had given his little sister.

Booker came back inside wearing a strange expression. "Well, the bad news is we won't be able to get Newt on murder charges."

"Why not?" Lizzie asked.

" 'Cause," he said, breaking into a grin. "I just got a call from the hospital. Tommy's awake."

Tommy was actually sitting up, sipping a cup full of ice chips and complaining about the fact that no one would bring him any real food. He looked pale, and the bandage around his head made him seem smaller somehow. But his grin was unchanged and his eyes crinkled with mischief.

"Guess I had you all a little worried, huh?"

"Nah, we knew you'd pull out of it," Booker said, feigning indifference. Tommy, disappointed, looked at me. "Bet *you* was worried."

"Who me? Never doubted you for a minute."

"Ah, come on now. They said I been out over a week. Coulda died, they said."

Erica took Tommy's hand and gave it a squeeze. "They're lying, kiddo. We were all worried, okay?"

"Oh." He looked around the room for confirmation, still a little confused. The doctor had said he might not remember things, that it might take a while before he regained all of his memory. But Tommy seemed to be doing pretty well, as far as I could tell. The nurse said that when he came to, the first thing out of his mouth was "Newt's in on it! Him and Buck!"

It had taken a lot of talking to convince him that there never had been any gold, that the whole thing had been a game.

"I don't get it, he said, scratching at the bandage on his head."

"That's okay, Tommy," Booker said. "Neither do we."

Tommy closed his eyes as if the effort of thinking it through were too much for him.

"We should go," Rosie whispered. She took Booker's hand and started for the door.

"Hey!" Tommy said, opening his eyes suddenly. "Who was the big winner in that chowder contest, anyway?"

Rosie smiled, her dark eyes glowing with pride.

"Well, Tommy," Booker said, putting his arm around Rosie. "My beautiful wife here got the blue ribbon. But I'd have to say the real winner was Cass." He winked at Erica.

Tommy looked confused again, but Erica helped

him out. She leaned over and kissed me tenderly on the cheek.

"For once the sheriff's got it wrong, Tommy," Erica said. "I was the real winner."

"Huh?" he said. And a minute later, "Oh." And then a smile, a truly radiant, Tommy Green smile. "I get it. Cool."

Epilogue

They were all at my place; the Bailey brothers, Booker and Rosie, Martha and Tina, Tommy, Lizzie and, of course, Erica. Bart had the barbecue going, promising a repeat performance of his *carne asada* and Rosie, after much begging on our part, had made her famed chili rellenos. Even Buck had insisted on springing for the beer and was doing his fair share of consuming it out on the deck.

"I still say we got lucky," Booker said. "If they hadn't started ratting on each other, all we'd have is the tape."

"Which, given the strings these guys can pull, a judge would probably rule inadmissible," Martha said.

"How'd you know they'd turn on each other?" Booker asked. It was another beautiful day, one of the last of summer. We were lounging on the front deck, sipping Coronas with lime, watching the sailboats race around the tip of the island.

"Something in the professor's book," I explained. "He said we're all predictable. That we are slaves to our weaknesses. Well, I figured out that the one weakness these guys had in common wasn't just their greed. It was their compulsion to win. And if they couldn't win, then they'd want to make sure no one else did either."

"So they took each other down with them," Erica said, nodding.

"Tanya Harding would've fit into their group real nicely," Martha said, laughing.

"The whole thing seems so devious," Rosie said, shaking her head. "Betting on human beings."

"Oh, I don't know. I can see how it could become addictive."

They looked up at me and I laughed.

"Okay, I confess. Just before I showed the film, I made a little bet with Erica. She said Newt would be the first one to lose it, and I said it would be Ginny Cathwaite."

"So who won?" Tommy asked.

"We both did," Erica said, smiling.

"What did you bet?"

Suddenly, Erica blushed and changed the subject.

"So did Ginny Cathwaite really kill her father?" she asked Martha.

"It sure looks like it. Once Newt knew we had him

cold on Tommy, he was eager to take Guy and Ginny down, too. It seems Guy made the mistake of bragging about it to Newt. According to Newt, their old man was loaded and they didn't feel like waiting for their share of the inheritance. Anyway, the one person that surprises me in all this is the professor."

"How so?" Rosie asked.

"You'd think he'd do everything he could to protect them, but he actually seems eager to cooperate."

"That doesn't surprise me," I said. "If Guy and Ginny go to jail, guess who's left with the money?"

"So he just gets off scot-free?" Rosie asked. "What about his conspiring to kill Buck? And Newt?"

Martha shrugged. "You know how hard it's going to be to get a conviction on conspiracy charges? A good lawyer will just say it was another game."

"Exactly," I said. "They can claim the whole thing was an act, that they knew all along they were being taped. They can say they were betting on how *we* would react — just another round of Seventh Heaven."

"Well, at least they won't be playing that game in our town anymore," Lizzie said. "Even if they do go free, they won't be welcome around here."

"Which one of 'em was putting up them bandanas and notes?" Buck wanted to know. Without the perpetual scowl, he didn't look so scary, I thought. In fact, the nose rings were starting to grow on me.

"Hawk and Guy took turns," Booker said. "Hawk couldn't wait to tell us all the details. You ever notice how some guys, once they're caught, just have to get it off their chest? Anyway, he says Guy put up the first two, then he put up the next two, then Guy did the last one. He says they made it like a treasure hunt. One of the bets they had going was how long you'd keep looking before you figured out it was all a joke."

"Real funny," Buck said. "Wait a minute. That's five. Three for Guy and two for the Hawk dude. Are you sure that's what he said?"

"I'm positive, Buck. I've got it written down somewhere. Plus it's on cassette tape. What's the matter?"

Buck had stood up and started pacing the deck. Beads of sweat stood out on his shiny pate. Then he started to laugh.

"What's up, bro?" Bart asked, looking worried.

"Dude! Ah, man. I'm gonna kill myself!"

"What?" Bart stood too.

"I'm a fucking idiot, is all. Sorry, ma'am," he said to Rosie. "Jesus, what a fucking idiot!"

"What?" Booker and I asked together.

"Damn! When I found out the whole thing was nothing but a joke, I tore up those notes and trashed them."

"So?" Bart prompted.

"So! There were six notes, man, counting the one Tommy took. Six! Not five. Don't you see!"

"You're saying you think one of them was real?" Tommy asked, his eyes lighting up.

The whole group fell silent, thinking about it.

"Wait a minute!" Bart said. "It's Saturday!" He started running down the ramp.

"Where are you going?" Tommy yelled, right on his heels.

"It's trash day. Come on. Maybe we can get there in time!"

"Oh, boy, here we go again," I said, watching the three of them jump into Tommy's boat and roar across the water.

"So much for the *carne asada*," Lizzie said, laughing.

"You don't think for a second he found the real note?" Martha asked.

"I don't even want to think about it. Anyone ready for a beer?" I walked inside to the kitchen and Martha followed me.

"So what *did* you two bet anyway?" she asked, grinning.

"Hmm?" I said, hiding my face in the refrigerator.

Erica came in and caught Martha's question.

"Whatever it was," she said, winking at Martha before taking me in her arms, "we plan on taking a long, long time to pay it off."

A few of the publications of
THE NAIAD PRESS, INC.
P.O. Box 10543 Tallahassee, Florida 32302
Phone (850) 539-5965
Toll-Free Order Number: 1-800-533-1973
Web Site: WWW.NAIADPRESS.COM
Mail orders welcome. Please include 15% postage.
Write or call for our free catalog which also features an incredible selection of lesbian videos.

MURDER UNDERCOVER by Claire McNab. 192 pp. 1st Denise Cleever thriller.	ISBN 1-56280-259-3	$11.95
EVERY TIME WE SAY GOODBYE by Jaye Maiman. 272 pp. 6th Robin Miller mystery.	ISBN 1-56280-248-8	11.95
SEVENTH HEAVEN by Kate Calloway. 240 pp. 7th Cassidy James mystery.	ISBN 1-56280-262-3	11.95
STRANGERS IN THE NIGHT by Barbara Johnson. 208 pp. Her body and soul react to a stranger's touch.	ISBN 1-56280-256-9	11.95
THE VERY THOUGHT OF YOU edited by Barbara Grier and Christine Cassidy. 288 pp. Erotic love stories by Naiad Press authors.	ISBN 1-56280-250-X	14.95
TO HAVE AND TO HOLD by Petty J. Herring. 192 pp. Their friendship grows to intense passion . . .	ISBN 1-56280-251-8	11.95
INTIMATE STRANGER by Laura DeHart Young. 192 pp. Ignoring Tray's myserious past, could Cole be playing with fire?	ISBN 1-56280-249-6	11.95
SHATTERED ILLUSIONS by Kaye Davis. 256 pp. 4th Maris Middleton mystery.	ISBN 1-56280-252-6	11.95
SETUP by Claire McNab. 224 pp. 11th Detective Inspector Carol Ashton mystery.	ISBN 1-56280-255-0	11.95
THE DAWNING by Laura Adams. 224 pp. What if you had the power to change the past?	ISBN 1-56280-246-1	11.95

These are just a few of the many Naiad Press titles — we are the oldest and largest lesbian/feminist publishing company in the world. We also offer an enormous selection of lesbian video products. Please request a complete catalog. We offer personal service; we encourage and welcome direct mail orders from individuals who have limited access to bookstores carrying our publications.

LOOKING FOR NAIAD?

Buy our books at
www.naiadpress.com

or call our toll-free number
1-800-533-1973

or by fax (24 hours a day)
1-850-539-9731